Seascapes

EVELYN GRACE

THREE STRANDS
PUBLISHING COMPANY

"A CORD OF THREE STRANDS IS NOT QUICKLY BROKEN." (ECC. 4:12B)

Seascapes

This novel is a work of fiction. The characters and events depicted are fictional and a product of the author's imagination. Any resemblance to actual characters, living or dead, locales, or events is coincidental.

Trade paperback ISBN 978-1-7345735-2-7
eBook AISN B089QQT4NC

All scripture quotations are taken from the New American Standard Bible® (NASB) Copyright © 1960, 1962, 1963, 1968, 1971, 1972, 1973, 1975, 1977, 1995 by the Lockman Foundation. Used by permission. www.Lockman.org

Cover design: © K&J Couture Designs
Cover photo: © Lisa-Anne Berry
Author photo: © Click and Capture Photography

For my Mom
Joyce Evelyn Gillespie

You are missed as much today as they day
you left. Thank you for giving me
my love of books.

For my Mom-in-Law
Trudy Grace Berry

Thank you for always loving me like a daughter.

Prologue

The young girl lay in the middle of the oversized hospital bed looking frail and small. Her tiny body barely made an imprint under the blankets covering her. An IV line ran from her left arm up to two bags hanging above her bed. Oxygen cannulas were fitted to her nose with tape holding them in place on each cheek. Her eyes were closed as if in sleep, but she wasn't sleeping. She had lots of practice faking sleep. She prayed this time it might keep her safe.

"It's okay, sweetie. This will make you feel better. Mommy knows more than these silly old doctors. Just hold still and let me give you this," a soft voice crooned at her bedside. "I never would have even brought you here if that nosy old biddy who lived next door had minded her own business. How could she ever know how much I love you?" The voice began to rise sharply.

The little girl stopped pretending to sleep and scrunched her eyes closed even tighter. Whenever her mommy talked like that, she never felt better, only worse. Her stomach was clenching in knots and her little fists were holding on to the covers of the bed as if they were the only things holding her world steady.

"There we go, sweetheart. All done. You are such a good girl. Such a good, good, girl."

She always tried to be good for her mommy, but it was hard when she had so few days when she felt well. She always seemed to be sick.

There was the sound of hurrying movements and the child peeked through cracked eyelids.

Entering the room, a nurse demanded, "Ma'am, what are you doing? What did you just put in your daughter's IV?"

"What are you talking about? I didn't do anything."

"We can see what goes on in this room on a closed-circuit monitor. I just saw you add something to your daughter's IV line."

"That's outrageous! I've been sitting here for days, caring for her, praying she finally gets better! I want only the best for my daughter. The care in this hospital is subpar to say the least. I'll be talking with the doctor about a transfer to Children's Hospital immediately."

It was obvious her mom had gone on the defense and quickly, as usual.

"This security officer is going to escort you out of here. We have reason to believe you have been harming your daughter." The nurse was scowling. The scowl scared the little girl. It was a scowl that let her know things would never be the same.

Chapter 1

The sun was making its way over the horizon, bathing the sky in varying shades of pink, yellow, and orange coming together in a breathtaking manner. All the colors blended to form a spectacular sunrise. The old sailor's rhyme of "red sky in the morning, sailor take warning" ran through Kate's head as she noticed the distinct red hue of the sky.

She brushed it off and determined not to worry about what the day would bring. After all, worrying about what happened next had never stopped the event from occurring.

The view along the boardwalk made her early mornings even more enjoyable. Kate had never been a morning person, but with the help of copious amounts of coffee, and this view, it was far more bearable.

She loved living on the coast of Maine. The quaint village of Haven had been the perfect choice for her when she had been looking to move. The quiet seaside town, with its boardwalk and sea wall, was the perfect mix of sea and sand.

She drew in deep breaths of the fresh salty air as she briskly made her way towards her store. Even after all this time, she still loved knowing she owned her own shop. It wasn't the biggest on the boardwalk, but it was all hers.

Taking occasional sips from her travel cup, she soaked in the peacefulness of the day. Her straight brown hair blew in her face and she tucked it behind her ears out of habit. All along the boardwalk, other businesses were getting ready to open as well. She knew the day would begin to feel busy, but for now, it was quiet, and she drank it in along with her coffee.

As she arrived at Seascapes, her small store, she began digging for her keys in her bottomless purse. She knew it was time to clean it out if she couldn't find her large key ring in less than two minutes.

Her mind began going over her massive to do list for the day to prepare for the upcoming summer tourist season. Inventory needed to be completed, so she could order new stock. She would also need to start interviewing for temporary help so they would be well trained before Memorial Day when out-of-staters began arriving in droves.

She had hired Nancy just a few weeks ago to get ahead of the rush. However, Nancy was sometimes too gruff with the customers. Kate had taken pity on her when she showed up looking for a job.

She wasn't like the typical summer help Kate hired. For one thing, she wasn't even close to being a teenager. Nancy had to be in her mid-60s, at least, although she appeared older with lines running across her face like hashmarks. Her grey hair was thinning, and she seemed to have a permanent scowl on her face.

Nancy looked like she had lived a hard life. After all, she was searching for a part-time job instead of enjoying retirement. Kate had felt badly for the woman and had ended up giving her a part-time position.

She was so focused on her mental list, and looking for her keys, she almost missed the small brown package wedged in the door handle.

That was odd. She knew it hadn't been there last night when she'd locked up. It was certainly too early in the morning for a delivery to have been made.

Curious, she pulled it free. It wasn't large. In fact, it was about the size of one of the jewelry boxes she used in the store. She looked it over for a mark of some type that would give her a clue as to its contents, or who had placed it there. There was nothing.

It was a simple package wrapped in plain brown paper tied with twine. There were no postal marks or any other indication as to how it had arrived at her door.

Tucking it into her purse, she finally managed to locate her keys and unlock the door. Walking into the store, Kate glanced around with contentment as she headed towards the front counter. The satisfaction of owning her own retail business still hadn't worn off.

Her store now had a firm place on the boardwalk after being open for the last two years. She enjoyed every aspect of running her own business and the joy of reaching her goal of being independent and self-sufficient made each day worth it.

Setting the package on the front counter next to the register where she could deal with it later, she headed to the back room to start getting ready for the day. The store wasn't due to open for another two hours, which would give her plenty of time to start working on inventory.

The deadline to order new merchandise was coming fast and one thing Kate disliked was missing a deadline. She thrived on routine. She enjoyed being focused on a task. Proficiency kept her busy and kept her mind from wandering.

Just as she had settled in behind her desk and was waiting for her computer to boot up, she heard a familiar thump at the back door. Hurrying over, she swung it open. Blowing in like a gale force wind, her only friend and full-time employee, Fiona Gilliam, came in carrying two cups of coffee.

Fiona was the type of person everyone wanted to be friends with. She was a vivacious woman of Irish descent, as her name attested. In stereotypical fashion, she had long curly red-hair and striking green eyes. She was taller than Kate at around five foot seven, but Fiona preferred wearing heels which gave her the illusion of more height.

"Good morning," Kate said with a wry smile on her face. She was quite used to the entrances Fiona liked to make. Secretly, she enjoyed them. Fiona was the opposite of Kate in every way from looks to manners and more. It was one of the countless reasons Kate enjoyed their friendship.

Kate wished she were as outgoing as Fiona at times. She also sometimes wished she were taller. She could barely claim five foot three inches. She loved her friend all the same even if they were as opposite as could be.

"Morning, sunshine! Here you go." Fiona handed Kate one of the steaming cups of coffee. "Your second cup, just the way you like it. It's going to be a glorious day today! Drink up and let's get this inventory done. Low tide is at noon today and you and me have a date in the tide pools. Last night's storm is sure to have brought in lots of sea glass."

Fiona was one of those people who enjoyed mornings, and Kate tried not to hold it against her. It really was a wonder they had ever become friends.

Ironically, it was a morning just like this that had brought them together. Kate had been trying to dig her keys out of her purse, like she did most mornings. Just as she had almost snagged them, she had fumbled her purse and ended up dumping the contents on the sidewalk. Fiona had been walking past and noticed her struggle.

She swept in, helped Kate find her keys, and picked up all her belongings. Then she had invited herself in. Fiona ended up helping Kate throughout the morning and before Kate realized what she was doing, she had offered Fiona a job.

She'd never had a friend before, not one who counted anyway or one who was always there for her. But there was something different about Fiona that had drawn her in. "Fee," as Kate affectionately called her, had managed to get past the defenses Kate had up. Kate hadn't regretted it yet.

"Fee, I'm not sure I can get away today. I have so much to do, not including the inventory. Nancy is still new and I'm not sure she's up to watching the store alone."

"Kate, listen. Nancy has been working here long enough. It's still early spring. At the ocean. It's cold if you haven't noticed. Mrs. Johnson will be the only one coming through to see how things are going. You know how she is. She could use a little snark directed at her and you know it."

Kate knew Fee was right. Her newer employee definitely had some snark to give out. "I need to talk to her today anyway about her attitude. If she continues to be so rude, she's going to drive away customers. I should also get some job postings listed and see if any of the local teens want to work here part-time for the busy season."

"Come on, Kate. You know there won't be enough customers to keep all three of us hopping today. We'll miss out on getting more sea glass and you know the inventory is low without even having to look at the stock we have on hand. Last night's storm will have dumped a bunch of glass. You know you want to come with me." Fiona finished with a bright smile on her face. She knew exactly what buttons to push.

"Okay, okay, okay. I'll go. You're right. You're always right."

"Of course I am, and don't you forget it!"

As they continued talking, they had wandered from the back room to the front of the store near the display windows. The space held a presentation of beautifully crafted sea glass jewelry draped artfully over pieces of driftwood. There were also some hung like light pendants, so they seemed to float in midair. It was the reason so many tourists, and even locals, came to Seascapes.

Kate and Fiona spent many hours during the fall and winter collecting sea glass from the beach and crafting their finds into necklaces, bracelets, and earrings.

They used locally sourced sea glass as much as they could. It meant more work to collect it, but Kate liked to use what they found. It leant authenticity to their pieces. It also meant they had more returning customers every year.

Seascapes also carried other items made by area residents. Pottery made from local clay, sculptures made from driftwood, and even photos of the surrounding towns added to the artistry of the display cases. Kate worked hard to support area artisans and as a result had a very eclectic display of products.

"Hey, what's this?" Fiona asked Kate. She held up the package Kate had left by the register.

"I'm not sure. It was wedged in the door when I opened this morning. I have no idea what it is."

"Mystery package, huh? Well, get the scissors and let's find out what's inside!" Fiona was always excited about life and mysteries. She was practically rubbing her hands together in anticipation.

It was another thing Kate loved about her friend. Life was never dull when she was around. As much as Kate enjoyed her solitude, she also loved spending time with Fee and seeing life through her eyes. She knew her own view of life was often more cynical.

Grabbing the scissors from the holder on the counter, Kate cut the twine. Unwrapping the paper, they found a simple box. Kate slit the tape holding it closed. Inside, amongst brown paper, was a cardboard jewelry box. The top of the box had the logo for Kate's store stamped on it. The two women exchanged puzzled glances as Kate slowly pulled the cover off the box.

Nestled inside, on a bed of cotton, was a necklace. It was obviously hand crafted. The necklace was made to display a beautiful piece of red sea glass. The glass had almost a heart shape to it. There was silver wire wrapped artfully around it, holding it in its setting. A simple, worn, silver chain was threaded through a loop in the top of the wire. Nothing else set it apart. In all actuality, other than the color of the glass, there was nothing unusual about the necklace aside from the way it had arrived at the shop.

"It's beautiful!" Fiona breathed. "Is there a note or something inside? I've never seen such a gorgeous piece of red glass before."

All the color had drained from Kate's face. Her normally pale complexion had managed to go even whiter. She was breathing shallowly, almost panting, on the verge of hyperventilating. Her eyes were wide, and she looked as if she might pass out at any moment.

Chapter 2

Peter sighed as he laid his head on the back of his chair. He had thought coming to Haven was what God wanted. When the opportunity had come up to help revitalize a dying church in a small Maine coastal town, he had thought it was perfect for him. It helped that he had wonderful memories of coming here with his family when he was a teenager. His parents always had a bunch of kids with them on those vacations.

Chuckling, Peter thought they must have made quite the sight when they showed up in town. They were always in some type of beat up van pulling an even more beat up trailer with supplies to last a week. Camping was cheap. The outside was free. The beach was a perfect place to let a lot of little ones run around, digging in the sand and boogie boarding on the waves.

It had made the long drive to and from Haven worth it. The time spent here camping was always fun, even when it rained. He remembered one year when it had seemed to do nothing but rain the entire time. It had taken him weeks after to finally feel dry.

It was the most fun some of the kids his parents cared for ever had in their lives. His parents had been foster parents when he was growing up. There were always kids coming and going from their house.

Some kids lasted a few days either for respite care or until their parents recovered from whatever had forced their removal in the first place. Others had stayed a few months and some had even stayed a few years. Then there were the others who had stayed forever.

His family had grown by four siblings during that time. He was sure it was only restraints on his parents' time that kept him from having more adopted siblings. His parents had always loved having kids of all ages and sizes around. They had a gift of relating to even the most hardened of hearts.

Now they showered it all on their many grandchildren. Given that Peter had seven siblings, biological and adopted, there were more than just a few grands around to spoil.

It was memories like those blissful days at the sea, which had made him jump at the chance to move to Haven. But had he jumped because he wanted to or because God wanted him to? He had thought he had been listening closely but maybe his own desire had gotten in the way.

Peter thought back again to the times when some of his foster siblings had arrived at their home. They had come with such sad faces, almost defeated, and often with all their belongings in a trash bag. Some had also come in with a look that said they'd seen far too much in their lives. Others had come ready for a fight. His parents always seemed to know how to handle each and every one.

He grinned as he thought of his brother. Drew had arrived at the Grant home not long before they had begun taking their vacations to Haven. He had been one of the ones who had shown up looking like he was ready to strike someone. He had been around fourteen when he arrived. Peter himself had been just older at sixteen.

Drew had arrived on the Grant doorstep with his trash bag and both fists clenched. Their home was the tenth Drew had been sent to. It was the last resort of the social worker, who had already given up on him.

Peter's parents refused to give up on Drew though. It had been a rough adjustment, but he was glad to be able to call Drew his brother and not just his foster brother. They were now best friends and Drew was another reason Peter had thought Haven was where he was supposed to be.

Drew had moved to Haven soon after figuring out college wasn't for him. He had originally gone to school for a degree in computer science but realized the desk style job wasn't for him. He had moved to Haven and started his own handyman business. He also volunteered time to help the church with maintenance.

Even though Peter had originally agreed to come to Haven to see if he could help revitalize the small church, it was really an excuse to be closer to Drew. And so far, helping the church had been a bust.

Peter sighed. He thought he had this "waiting for God" and "trusting the Lord" thing down. He thought he knew how to communicate with God. He thought he knew a lot of stuff. But sometimes it felt like God threw a curve ball at him.

Some church members were still mourning the passing of their long-time pastor who had died suddenly one morning of a heart attack in the middle of his sermon. It was taking them a long time to come to terms with the fact that Pastor Dan was gone, and Pastor Peter was now here.

Peter closed his eyes and began to have another conversation with God. There was obviously something he was missing in all of this. He prayed God would make it known so he would know how to proceed.

"Hey, dreaming on the job again?"

As if thoughts of his brother had conjured him up, Peter's eyes flew open and he jerked his head up to see Drew standing in the doorway.

"Dreaming how I ever agreed to let you talk me into this. You know, you could have warned me about the congregation."

"Not this again. Come on, little brother, they aren't that bad. And you know it's not my fault you're here." Drew crossed the room and dropped into the chair in front of the desk.

"I'm not your little brother, and you know it. Stop calling me that." Peter always became slightly irked at the nickname. It wasn't his fault he could barely claim five foot ten while Drew was a giant at six foot three.

"When it stops being true, I'll stop saying it." A wide grin covered Drew's tanned face. He knew exactly what buttons to push to get a reaction. He always had.

Drew and Peter were opposite in looks as well. While Peter was slender with dark hair, he kept cut short, and dark eyes, Drew had a more solid build. He was blonde with slightly shaggy hair, and bright blue eyes. It was like he was meant to live in a beach-side community.

"What's bugging you now?" Drew reached out and grabbed a paperclip off the desk. He always had a hard time sitting still. He bounced the clip between his palms and then started to unbend it and bend it back.

"The usual, I guess. How am I supposed to reach these people when they don't want me here? Should I even be here? I'm starting to wonder if God had other plans for me and I was too blind to see them."

"I would think you would know how to talk to people. You know, have those hard conversations." Drew grabbed another paperclip from the desk to mangle. "Didn't Mom and Dad teach you anything?" He threw the clip at Peter's head.

Peter reached out and snatched it before it smacked him in the forehead. He had tried all the things he knew to win people over.

He had done home visits. Some of the congregants had only reluctantly allowed him access. Others had outright denied him. He had kept his sermon topics light instead of delving into harder ones. It just wasn't working.

"Tell me more about Agnes Johnson." She seemed to be the matriarch of the congregation. Peter felt if he could win her over, he could, perhaps, get everyone else on board with him staying.

"Why don't you jump in the Atlantic and swim to England instead?" Drew shot Peter a look that let him know he was in for a battle. "She thinks her way is the only way. Although, maybe if you flirted with her a bit, that would work."

Drew barked out a laugh, ducking as Peter chucked the paperclip back across at him.

Chapter 3

Kate! Here, sit down!" Fiona hurried Kate behind the counter to sit on a stool. She grabbed a paper bag from underneath and fashioned it so that Kate could breathe into it. She held it in front of her friend's face. "Breathe slowly."

Kate obeyed simply because she didn't have the strength to do anything else. Gradually, the panic started to subside. Her breathing began to return to normal. Her racing heart slowed enough that she thought it would agree to stay in her chest.

"Better?" Concern for her friend was etched across Fiona's face.

Kate still didn't feel up to speaking, so she just nodded her head as she continued to work on her breathing. Breathe in. Breathe out. Breathe in. Breathe out. If she just concentrated on getting air into her lungs, she wouldn't have to think about anything else.

"I'm guessing you know something about this." Fiona glanced at where the necklace was sitting on the counter. She didn't want to prod Kate for information right now, but curiosity about the situation was starting to overwhelm her. Fee asked with caution, "Do you want to talk about it?"

"No. Not now. Not ever. Get rid of it. Toss it back in the ocean. I never want to see it again!" Kate could barely get the words out. She still didn't seem to have quite enough air in her lungs to talk freely.

Fee looked surprised. Kate had never once lost her temper in all the time they had known each other. Not even when Mrs. Johnson came in with her over the top demands. "Just concentrate on breathing. We'll talk about it in a minute. Do you want something to drink?"

Nodding again, Kate closed her eyes and continued to focus on getting air into her lungs. It shouldn't take this much concentration just to breathe.

She didn't want to start thinking about what the necklace being here could mean. Instead, she continued to put all her attention on getting more air. Thinking would only make it worse. She didn't want to remember. She didn't want to feel. She just wanted to be left alone to live her life. She didn't want this! She had never wanted any of it.

Why had the necklace shown up here? And, more importantly, *how* had the necklace shown up here? She had thought it was gone forever.

Carrying a bottle of water, Fiona pulled up a second stool. "I've never seen red sea glass before." Fiona began speaking in a soft tone. "I have to assume it's pretty rare."

"It is. That's the only piece I've ever seen in my life." Kate could feel her heart starting to return to normal and her breathing coming easier. "Fee, I really don't want to talk about this right now. I'm feeling better. Let's just get started on the inventory so we can go hunt for sea glass later. I promise, I'm okay."

"I've never asked about your past, and you've never told me, but I'd be a fool not to realize there's something going on here. And since you've never told me much about your life before you showed up in Haven, I'm betting this necklace has something to do with your past. Am I right?"

Kate nodded her head quickly in assent. Yes, the necklace had something to do with her past. Something she thought was long over. Something she never thought she'd have to deal with again.

"I'm not going to push you to tell me about it now, but I really think we should discuss whatever this is about at some point. Agreed? And some point soon."

Fiona had that look about her, which meant she wasn't going to let Kate push it off. Fee could be stubborn at times and Kate knew this would be one of those times.

With a sigh so deep it seemed to come from the soles of her feet, Kate once more agreed with her friend's statement. "Okay. Probably. Maybe. It's not that I don't want to tell you, Fiona. I'm just not sure I can. You're right, but not now. Please, just get rid of it. I really don't want to see it ever again."

With a look of resignation, Fiona picked up the box and wrappings and headed to the office. Kate sipped on the water bottle and looked once more at the display in the window. It seemed as if her past had managed to catch up with her. Sighing deeply once more, she pushed the hard memories to the back of her mind, where they belonged.

Chapter 4

The doctor gently pulled Mrs. Winters aside and tried to usher her into an empty room nearby. The look of concern on his face made her begin to talk rapidly and she seemed rooted to the spot.

"Doctor, I brought her in as soon as I could! Is she going to be okay? Is my baby going to be alright?" She nearly shrieked at him as she grabbed his arm in panic. Her other hand clenched her older daughter, towing her beside her.

Kate didn't understand what was happening. What was wrong with her baby sister? Why was her mom yelling so much?

The doctor hadn't wanted to have this conversation in the hallway, in full view of everyone, but the woman had ambushed him outside her daughter's room. She refused to be budged and seemed not to care about disturbing other patients or staff.

"I'm sorry, Mrs. Winters. We've tried everything we possibly could." He gently pried her fingers off his forearm. "I just don't understand. She isn't responding to any of the normal treatments. You'll want to contact your husband to come in to say good-bye. I'm so sorry." The doctor shook his head slightly as he turned to walk away.

Mrs. Winters began to cry. Tears rolled down her face as she began to shriek at him, "No! Please, no! Doctor! I just can't lose my sweet Lori! There must be something else you can do! There has to be!"

Kate sat bolt upright in bed. Panting hard, she moved to the edge and sat, waiting for her racing heart to quiet. She had few memories of her younger sister, Lori.

She had only been five years old at the time and hadn't understood what was going on. Her sister had been three years younger. Much later she had learned why, and how her sister had died, and that she had almost experienced the same fate.

Her father used to scream at Kate how it was all her fault when he was in one of his drunken rages. He never told her a reason why but would always blame her all the same. He had blamed Kate not only for Lori's death, but everything with her mother as well. Even after all this time, after all the therapy, and after all the changes Kate had made to her life, her past still seemed to keep a tight grip on her and refused to let go.

She pushed the covers aside and went to the bathroom to get a drink of water. Staring at her reflection, she couldn't help but wonder why. Why had she survived but her sister hadn't? She thought she'd already figured all this out with her therapist when she was younger, but apparently not.

It was the necklace. That awful necklace!

She may not remember her sister, but she certainly remembered the necklace. It had always hung around her mother's neck. Always. She never thought she'd see it again.

Kate walked back to her room and continued out the door to the living room. She didn't think she'd get any more sleep tonight. Maybe a hot cup of chamomile tea would help her relax.

As she moved around the kitchen, her mind wandered back to the conversation she'd had with Fiona while they'd been hunting for sea glass that afternoon.

"Kate, what's up with the necklace? Are you going to tell me about it or keep me guessing?" Fiona had prodded her relentlessly while they combed the beach. If there is one thing Fiona hated more than anything, it was being left in the dark. Kate knew she would continue to nag her about the necklace until she had dragged all the details out.

Kate felt like all she had done today was sigh as another one filled her lungs. "I just don't like talking about it, Fiona. It all happened a long time ago and I thought it was over. I never thought I'd see it again. I've been trying to leave the past in the past where it belongs."

But Fee wasn't content to leave it alone. "Well, do you at least know who it belonged to?"

"It was my mother's." Kate had continued walking after stating this simple fact. She kept scanning the beach for a twinkle to indicate sun glistening off glass.

So far this morning they'd found quite a few pieces of brown, green, and white sea glass, which were the most common colors. There were even some similar enough in size to be made into earrings. She was hoping to find a few more and perhaps even a few blue ones.

Blue glass was rare, but she had found some over the years. She had one large piece from a few months ago she was planning to make into a necklace. If she could find two smaller ones, she could make earrings for a set.

"Is that all you're going to tell me? It was your mother's? Honestly, Kate. Don't you trust me enough at this point to share your life with me?"

Kate thought about her answer for a moment. She held back the sarcasm which would have been her normal defensive response. Fiona was the first person in years she had ever let past some of her walls. She had learned long ago it was better to never rely on anyone. They always let you down or hurt you. But Fiona was different. She had always proved herself to be trustworthy.

She also knew Fiona had a wonderful relationship with her parents, who lived just a few towns away. Kate had even spent time with them during the holidays once Fee realized she usually spent them alone.

Fee had a family who loved her, and she loved them. It was obvious in the way she talked about them. Kate didn't begrudge her this. She wasn't even jealous, not at this point in her life. It just made it harder to explain things. Fee would have nothing to compare it to.

Kate sighed, "Fee, my family was nothing like yours. Just leave it alone. My mother didn't love me. She just loved the attention having children gave her, but she certainly didn't love me. I don't want any reminder of her and that is what the necklace is to me. A reminder of something I want to forget. Just leave it be, okay?"

To her credit, Fee had done just that. She had stopped pestering Kate while the two continued searching for sea glass. Kate had walked home from the beach trying hard not to keep thinking about her past.

She had begun a cleaning frenzy as soon as she returned home. It was how she coped when things just seemed so far out of control. From a young age, whenever she had become scared or angry, she would start scrubbing every surface she could find.

Standing now in her sparkling kitchen in the dark hours of the morning, Kate tried hard to stop her spinning thoughts. How had the necklace ended up at the shop? More importantly, *why* did it arrive? Had her father found her? Did her father even have the necklace in his possession? She had never seen him with it.

While she hadn't tried hard to cover her tracks when she'd left home, she had never dreamed he would come after her. He hadn't wanted to be a part of her life when she had lived with him, so she couldn't fathom he had changed enough that he would want to see her now. Most likely he thought he could get some money out of her to pay off his latest gambling debt.

She grabbed her mug and headed to the living room. Curling up on one end of the couch and pulling a blanket over herself, she began to sip her tea. Her mind raced as thoughts of her past continued running through her mind.

Setting down her half-finished drink on the small table beside her, she closed her eyes and began to take deep breaths. In and out. Just like her therapist had shown her. It had been years since she had fought anxiety, but tonight it seemed to be winning the battle. In and out. In and out. Slowly, slowly she could feel herself relaxing as she forced her thoughts into submission. Kate finally pulled in one last deep breath and drifted off into a fitful sleep.

Chapter 5

Drew laughed again to himself as he remembered the look on Peter's face when he suggested he flirt with Agnes Johnson. That would definitely be something he would pay to watch. The town matriarch knew how to make everyone do her bidding. And she wouldn't put up with anything like that from Peter or anyone else either. Another laugh slipped out as Drew continued walking.

She currently had decided Peter was not up to her standards of a "proper pastor" as she put it. What she failed to remember was Pastor Dan had also started at the church as a young man, younger even than Peter. Drew had looked it up in the church records.

He would give her another few weeks to come around before he went to speak with her. He had learned during his time living in Haven that it was best to allow Mrs. Johnson to change her mind without letting on anyone had helped her do it. She liked to think she was in charge.

Drew just enjoyed watching his brother squirm a bit. He wasn't planning to let the church fail because the old woman couldn't accept his brother as a pastor. Pastor Dan had been an excellent minister, but so was Peter. Peter was just having a hard time believing it at the moment.

Drew whistled to himself as he strolled along the boardwalk. He had gone for his usual morning jog. The chilly air was welcomed. It had a hint of summer behind it. Soon it would be hard to have the beach to himself in the morning. It would be teeming with tourists in just a few weeks.

The six-mile run had been just what he needed to clear his head. His breakup with Lucy hadn't gone as he had hoped. But then, no breakup ever really did, did it?

It turned out she was one of those crying, clingy ones who begged him to change his mind. He should have known. She had been a crying, clingy woman when they were dating, too.

It wasn't that he didn't like Lucy. She was nice enough. She was definitely gorgeous enough. It was just that he couldn't see himself settling down with her. He couldn't picture her caring for children. Heck, he wasn't even sure he could picture her having kids. And he wanted kids of his own one day.

The Grants had shown him how much fun it was to have lots of kids to love. He wanted lots of his own one day. One day, when he found the right woman, if he ever did. He knew he needed to trust God to bring just the right person into his life, but sometimes he wasn't sure it was ever going to happen.

He was starting to get to the point where he was feeling his age. He was looking thirty square in the face, and he didn't always like what he saw. The lack of a wife and children was one of the things he was beginning to feel a tug about. A big tug.

He continued his walk toward home as he cooled down from his run. Well, being honest with himself he hadn't walked directly home because he had stopped at the Three Cat Café to get a cup of coffee. Fine, and a cinnamon roll. It was worth every mile he ran to sink his teeth into the yummy goodness of the pastry. They baked them every Wednesday and he was usually one of the first in line after they opened to snag one. Alright, maybe two.

He tore off a bite of his roll and almost groaned out loud at the taste. It was delicious. He wiped his mouth on the sleeve of his sweatshirt. Then he quickly glanced around to be sure no one had seen him. His parents had certainly taught him better manners than he was currently displaying.

His parents. He knew how blessed he had been to land on the Grant's doorstep. His social worker had warned him if he didn't straighten up and fit into this family, that was it. He would be heading to a halfway house instead.

The last guy had tried, Drew gave him credit for that. He certainly hadn't made it easy for him either. Drew had done everything he could to sabotage every family placement he had been put in. He was a stubborn kid who just wanted to go *home*. But home wasn't an option anymore.

Then he had met the Grants and realized home could be a place where you were loved when you couldn't go back to where you had started. They had loved him so hard and relentlessly that he didn't have any more excuses. He had finally let down his walls and allowed himself to feel wanted once more. He had become part of a family again, something he never thought would happen.

Taking another bite of his second cinnamon roll, he shook off the thoughts of the past. He tried not to think about the years before he became a Grant. They were too painful. He didn't want to let those memories disrupt his day.

Sipping on his cooling coffee, he decided to head to the church before he went home. Peter would probably be there. He could check to see if there was anything he could help him with.

The small church had no budget for a maintenance or janitorial crew. It was just Peter. The deacons and elders were almost as ancient as Mrs. Johnson. Drew had started helping out long before Peter arrived and continued to do so. He had the skills and enjoyed working with his hands.

His small handyman business allowed him the freedom of a flexible schedule. It also allowed him to help the church when they needed it.

Sure enough, he saw lights on in the office. Peter was already there. He was either working on his sermon for the week or planning out his next stage of attack to win over Mrs. Johnson and the rest of the Pastor Dan contingent at church.

Drew eased open the door to the hallway just outside Peter's office. He shut the door quietly and tiptoed towards his brother's office thinking of a way to surprise him. He stopped short, however, when he heard voices coming from behind the slightly opened door.

Drew glanced at his watch. It was just after seven in the morning, but he would know that voice anywhere. Mrs. Johnson was here meeting with his brother, and it sounded like they had already been at it for a while.

"Now, as to the song selections, I think that is the next important thing to address. None of this modern racket. Just an organ or a piano or perhaps both. No other instruments are needed."

She let out a loud sniff before she continued with laying out her edicts for Peter. "Good old-fashioned hymns are what we have always sung. That is what we should continue to do. I would be happy to pick out the songs each week. I'm sure that will make things easier."

He risked a peek around the door. Sure enough, Peter had a harried look about him. He had his fists clenched on top of the desk. He was probably trying not to strangle old Mrs. Johnson.

Peter looked up and caught sight of Drew craning his neck around the door. He arched an eyebrow. Drew shot him a look and shook his head. No way was he going in there and facing Mrs. Johnson in his shorts and sweatshirt. Even he wasn't that brave.

Smiling at his brother, he shook his head firmly in the negative and backed away. He would go sit in the sanctuary and wait there.

"Young man, are you listening to me?"

Drew's shoulders shook as he contained his laughter. Mrs. Johnson was in rare form this morning. He grinned as he devoured another bite of his third cinnamon roll. The mileage on his run this morning was worth the extra pastries. He settled into a pew to wait for his brother. Poor Peter.

Chapter 6

Kate was sitting at her desk at the store going over invoices. She enjoyed the bookwork needed to run her business. It was orderly. She liked order. It was logical. There was a start and a finish to it, a quiet peace once all the pieces fit.

Summer always seemed to arrive fast, so she needed to make sure they had plenty of products on hand. She made a note to contact the local artisans and ensure they would be able to fill orders. She would also need to renew contracts with those who would be returning.

She was on autopilot. Her thoughts were completely focused on the business at hand. She didn't want to think about anything other than making Seascapes successful for another year. She shoved thoughts of the past to the back of her mind. She didn't want to feel the pain again. Not now.

Fiona walked briskly in through the back door. "Hey! How are you doing today?" Concern was laced through her voice as she handed Kate a cup of coffee.

"I'm fine, Fee. Let's just focus on what we need to get done today." Kate sipped her coffee and turned the conversation immediately to store matters. "Do you think we have enough sea glass for the start of the summer? Do you think you'll have time to get some pieces made today?" Kate's questions were a rapid-fire redirection. She refused to continue talking about her feelings.

"Kate, I think you're going to have to talk about this more at some point. You can't hide from the fact a necklace from your past showed up at your store, out of the blue, hand-delivered even! Don't you find it strange?"

Kate shot Fiona a withering glance. "I'm not doing this right now, Fee. I'm just not." Standing up she grabbed her jacket and headed for the door. "I'll be back later."

"Hey! Don't leave angry. Let me help!"

Kate bolted for the door. While she could hear the concern and confusion in her friend's voice, she didn't want to explain anything right now. She just wanted to leave.

It had been years since Kate had become this angry this fast. Normally she was a calm person, but when she was younger, it seemed she could go from calm to boiling mad in an instant. She could feel the white-hot rage pulsing through her veins as the adrenaline began to hit her limbs and the shaking began.

"Kate! You can't just run off," Fiona chased after her. "You need to talk about this. We need to figure this all out! What could it mean?"

Whirling around, Kate's voice began to rise as she felt the tentative hold she had on her emotions breaking. "Don't you get it? I don't care! My past is just that, past. It doesn't affect me here and now. I won't let it!" She grabbed her purse from the bench near the door and stormed out.

Fiona watched her friend slam the door behind her. She had never known Kate to lose her cool like that before. There was more to this story about her mother's necklace. Fee just hoped Kate would allow her to help figure it out before it tore her friend apart.

◊ ◊ ◊ ◊ ◊

Feet pounding on the sidewalk, Kate headed down the street. She didn't care where she was going, she just knew she needed to get away. She needed to calm down. She hated when she lost her temper. She always felt so out of control when it happened and being in control was where she was most comfortable. It was where she felt most safe.

Being in control was how she managed to stay alive as a child. Being in control was how she worked full-time and went to high school, completing the college prep honors program, and graduating valedictorian. Being in control was how she graduated from college with a degree in business management and saved the money needed to start her store. Being in control was how she ended up where she was today. Being in control worked.

She wasn't about to give it up just so her father could appease his conscience or pay off his latest gambling debt. If it was even him who had delivered the necklace. It couldn't be him, but who else could it be? She hadn't told him where she was going when she had left. He wouldn't have gone to this much trouble to find her. Would he?

Kate looked up and noticed an old stone church tucked away on the corner just up ahead. She altered her course and headed towards it. She had never noticed it before, but it was almost hidden behind a line of trees off Main Street.

It was in the opposite direction from where she lived. She really hadn't taken a lot of time to just explore the town, other than the beach and boardwalk near where she lived. Staying in control also meant keeping reliable patterns to her days, and not seeking out new adventures.

As she walked closer to the quaint church, she thought maybe she could find some much needed quiet inside to just sit and pull herself together. She walked up the steps and tugged at the door. She assumed it would be locked, but to her surprise the door opened smoothly without even a squeak.

Pausing for a moment to let her eyes adjust after the brightness of the outside, she looked around. She found herself in a small atrium with double doors propped open in front of her leading into the sanctuary.

To her right was a tight spiral staircase leading upward. A thick rope was hanging beside it. Stepping forward, she peered up and saw a bell. She smiled at the sight of it. Every church should have a bell like this, she thought to herself.

As she continued forward through the doors into the sanctuary, she saw it was filled with rows of hard-backed pews. They at least had padded cushions on the seats. A slight upgrade made in the last fifty years, no doubt.

There was no center aisle. Instead, there was one to the left and one to the right, with a set of pews running right down the middle. Flanking each aisle was a smaller section of pews on either side. Beautiful stained-glass windows ran down each outside wall of the church. There were eight total, four on each side.

Kate walked slowly down the left side of the church gazing at the windows, studying each intently. The artistry was breathtaking. She had a vague knowledge of the Bible stories they depicted.

When she was little, after things had gone sideways with her parents, she had lived with a foster family. They had taken her to church with them. They had spent quite a bit of time at church, going every Sunday morning for Sunday school and church, every Sunday evening, and every Wednesday evening. She hadn't minded going with them at the time, yet it had been years since she had last stepped foot in a church.

There was a window showing the story of the birth of Jesus. It showed a picture of the baby in a manger with Mary and Joseph huddled over him and angels in the distant sky.

The next window showed a shepherd standing in a field with a lamb wrapped around his shoulders. The rest of the flock was on a hill behind them. The small plaque attached beneath the photo simply said, "The Ninety-Nine."

"Can I help you?"

Kate gasped and whirled. Seated at the back of the church on the opposite side from her was a man. He was holding a cup of coffee and was dressed in shorts and a sweatshirt. She hadn't noticed him when she arrived intent as she had been on the windows.

"I'm sorry! I just needed a quiet place to think. The door was open. I just thought…" Kate's voice trailed off as she stammered and stuttered her reply. She felt a slight flush of embarrassment coming over her checks. "I'll just leave."

Rising he came towards her. "No, please stay. It's not a problem. The church is always left open during the day. Sit down." He gestured to a pew. "Let me just go see if my brother is available. I'm assuming you want to speak with him?" Without waiting for Kate's reply, he turned and hurried through a door near the front.

Kate slid into a pew next to the shepherd window. She gazed up at it and quietly did some of her deep breathing exercises. A feeling of peace slowly began to come over her. Looking at all the details depicted in the window, she was reminded of the calm she used to feel while sitting in church with her foster family.

She heard the door open and a different man walked through. This one was shorter than the first, and as dark as the other had been light. He was dressed casually in a button-down shirt and khaki pants.

"Hello, I'm Pastor Peter. What can I do for you?"

"I'm sorry. I just needed a moment. Your church is beautiful. These windows are gorgeous."

Nodding towards the window she was sitting beside, he asked, "Do you know the story?"

Kate shook her head. She was hoping he wouldn't stay long. She just needed a few more moments alone to get back under control. She knew she would need to go back to the store and make amends with Fiona. She had never lost her temper with her before. Poor Fee had looked a little shell-shocked when Kate bolted.

He began to speak quietly and gently, sensing Kate's mood and need for peace. "Jesus used stories to teach. Many people couldn't read or write, and paper was a valuable commodity as the process to create it was a bit more involved back then. Stories were shared by mouth. Instead of sitting around and watching television, people would gather and share stories."

Kate had never thought of that before. She looked back at the window and began to wonder what it would have been like to live in a time when paper was scarce. She had shelves of journals. It was one way she had learned to cope with her emotions, by spilling them onto paper.

The man continued, "This particular story was about a shepherd. There were a lot of shepherds in those days so many people could easily relate. That's why Jesus shared stories like this. They always held some truth to them, something he was trying to teach the people. However, if he just shared the truth, many more would have rejected him immediately."

Kate wished he would finish up, but she didn't want to be rude. She just wanted to sit and think, not listen. She tried to mentally encourage him to hurry up, but he continued at the same steady pace.

"The shepherd in our story had one hundred sheep. It was his job to keep them safe from predators. He kept a close eye on them and would count them every morning and evening to be sure they were all gathered close. His entire livelihood was tied up in his flock.

They would feed his family and make sure they had everything they needed. It was his savings account."

Kate wondered how smelly sheep were in real life. She was pretty sure she preferred her money in the bank. Easier to control and less odor. Sheep had to stink, didn't they? She turned her attention back to the man.

"One day when he was counting, he found he only had ninety-nine sheep. He was missing one. He quickly began searching. He was frantic to find the one lost sheep. He called, knowing if it could hear his voice, it would come to him.

"Some would scoff that it would be foolish to leave the remaining ninety-nine sheep to go look for just one. Why bother? He had so many others, what was the life of this one sheep? Yet he continued to look. He loved all his sheep. They were all precious to him."

He stopped and looked up at the stained-glass window and Kate's eyes followed. A soft smile came to his lips. Kate had a vague sense of deja vu, as if she had heard this very man tell this story to her before. Shaking her head slightly at the nonsense of the thought, she looked back at him as he continued.

"After much searching, he found his lost sheep. He placed the sheep on his shoulders around his neck, just like the window shows, and returned to his flock. He even went back to his neighbors and friends and invited them to come celebrate with him. He was so overjoyed to have found his lost sheep."

Kate wondered if anyone would ever look for her like that. She had always lived her life not relying on anybody. She wasn't sure anyone would even notice if she went missing. Well, maybe Fiona, but certainly no one else.

But someone had found her, she thought to herself as she remembered the mysterious package left at the shop door. Who had taken the time to search for her? And why leave the necklace? Why hadn't they just come in the store?

She pulled her thoughts under control. It wasn't going to help. There was no use dwelling on the past and trying to figure it out. It didn't change the fact the necklace was there, and she was no closer to figuring out who had left it.

"Jesus used this story to show much He loves us and values us. Each person is just as important to Him as the next. He doesn't have favorites. He loves all of His children equally and will pursue each one just as the shepherd did his lost sheep."

The man stopped talking again. Kate sat in the silence, beginning to feel a bit uncomfortable as it lengthened.

Clearing his throat, he rose. "I can see you have a lot on your mind. Please, feel free to sit and pray and just enjoy the church. I'll be straightening things up out back. If you need anything, just ask."

Chapter 7

Kate watched in amazement as the man suddenly stood and headed back out the door he had entered through. She had been sure he was going to start preaching at her once he finished his story. She wasn't sure how she would have reacted. After all, it was obvious God had turned his back to her. What kind of God let a child die like her sister had anyway? What kind of God would permit the suffering she had experienced as a child?

And it was the sins of others, not her own, that caused her so much distress. She would never forgive what her mother and father had done to her as a child. They didn't deserve forgiveness. She had been too young to do anything to make things different, to make them better. She couldn't make things right. She couldn't have protected her little sister, and no one could bring Lori back.

She was not going to let her past continue to dictate her life. She just wanted to forget it. Just forget all of it. She certainly couldn't change it. How could she? Her mother was dead. Her father was gone.

So, where had the necklace come from? It seemed like all she had been doing for the past few days was think about her past and that necklace. She was just so tired of it all.

Reaching up, she rubbed her forehead. She wanted the past to stay buried, like it had been. She felt like her head would explode. Even now, she could feel the veins in her temples pounding. She switched to using both hands to try to rub away the growing pain.

When she had left to go to college, she had cut all ties. The pain she had endured as a child had become unbearable. When she had been forced to leave her foster family and go back to her father, she'd stopped going to therapy as well. While the counseling she had received as a child had helped, she'd still struggled with nightmares.

She had started back to regular therapy sessions when she was in college. Her nightmares made it impossible for her to share a room, so the school had insisted she figure it out since they were footing her bill. It was almost a month of sessions before she would even open up to the therapist about what had happened to her.

Even then, Kate had only been interested in learning how to keep it in the past rather than "processing through it" to find "healing" as the therapist had suggested. How was she supposed to "heal" from the fact that neither of her parents had loved her? That her own mother had harmed her? That her father had all but abandoned her?

Sitting in the pew, she continued rubbing her temples. Kate thought back to one therapy session. She had been seeing the counselor on campus for about four months.

She had finally given the therapist permission to get copies of all her old medical records. There were volumes of them sitting on her desk when Kate had arrived for their session. It was obvious Ms. Williams had been spending quite a bit of time with them. Bright pink sticky notes bristled like porcupine quills poking out in all directions from the stack.

"Kate," Ms. Williams had begun in her somewhat nasally tone, "let's start today by discussing your relationship with your father."

"Why? I haven't been having nightmares about him. I'm having nightmares about losing my sister. A sister I have so few memories of." Kate always found these sessions somewhat annoying. If the school weren't forcing her to attend and if she didn't need the scholarship money to continue, she would have stopped after the first session.

"Well, research has shown the degree of stress a child feels as an adult can relate back to how they were treated by their parents, in their formative years."

With biting sarcasm, Kate had shot back, "Let's see then. My mother used me to fuel her sick addiction for attention. She killed my sister before anyone could figure out what she was doing to us. She made me so ill I almost died, twice. No one knew what she was capable of, until it was too late. We were too small to defend ourselves, and no one else stepped up to help."

Kate had continued as she felt her heart rate rise along with her anger over the futility of it all. "And my father was either out drinking, gambling, or both. He certainly wasn't home to protect my sister or me. So, if you think the stress I felt as a child might be causing my nightmares, I agree wholeheartedly! I just need a way to deal with it! I need to finish my degree and I need the scholarship money to do it!"

Ms. Williams had always talked in a quiet voice. Kate had begun to hate that voice. It was always so composed when she had felt anything but calm. "Have you ever thought about letting go of what your parents did instead of holding on to it so tightly?"

Kate had been too shocked to reply for a moment. She was not holding on to it. It was holding on to her. She had felt the blood pulsing through her body, and she had begun to shake with rage. "I'm not holding on to it! Are you as crazy as my mother? My mother killed my sister! She starved her to death. She was only two years old. A baby! She injected so many poisons in my body that I don't even know if I'll ever have my own children. You must know that little fact from reading my medical records!"

Kate breathed deeply and continued to focus on the window. The shepherd had a knowing and gentle smile, like he had a secret. Maybe Fiona was right. Maybe it was time to bring all these memories up and deal with them. Ignoring them all these years hadn't done anything. The moment the past showed up, she found herself right back in the thick of it. Panic attacks hovering, just waiting to hit.

She forced herself to remember the rest of what she had spewed at Ms. Williams that day. "As for my father, he didn't protect me when I was young. Then he showed up out of the blue and ripped me away from the only family who ever truly cared for me."

She took a moment to try to gain some control, but it was no use. She was raging mad and continued to rant at her therapist.

"Once he had accomplished that, he abandoned me again, but this time, I had no one to help me. He would show up every few weeks and pay some bills and the rent, if I was lucky. I was left to raise myself in a place that wasn't safe for young girls."

Kate had sat shaking. How *dare* this woman, this person who had absolutely no idea what Kate's childhood had been like, even suggest such a thing. Kate hadn't held on to any of it, but the grip the past had on her refused to loosen its hold.

"Kate, I'm not condoning what your parents did to you. I'm talking about letting it go. I'm talking about not letting what they did continue to dictate your actions. Think about possibly forgiving them. It's about taking all the negative energy you are using to continue being mad at your parents and just letting it go."

Kate pulled in another shuddering breath. And then another. She focused again on the shepherd's smile. It helped as she began to force herself to relax bit by bit. If only it had been as easy as Ms. Williams made it seem that day. Just let it go.

Kate hadn't been able to do it. Her counselor had helped her figure out ways to deal with her stress and anxiety though. One method was spending time outside in nature, which is one reason she settled on living near the ocean. She didn't mind the cold Maine winters and there were very few days she couldn't get out at least once a day no matter the weather. A few layers were usually enough to make it comfortable.

Gathering up her purse and jacket, Kate rose. She needed to get back to the store and finish up the invoicing and orders. More importantly, she needed to apologize to Fiona for the way she had stormed out.

"Thank you for coming. Feel free to come back whenever you need a moment to gather your thoughts. The church is open every day." The voice floated towards Kate from the front of the church.

Kate stopped and looked back to see Pastor Peter was standing near the door he had disappeared through earlier. She wondered where the blonde man had disappeared to. There had been something intriguing about him, but she shook off the thought. She did not need any other complications in her life right now.

"Thank you. I may just be back. I like this church. It reminds me of the one I attended when I was little."

Kate hadn't realized it until she said it, but it was true. It wasn't just being in a church that had felt familiar, but this church was laid out in a similar way to the one she had attended with her foster family. It had felt comforting the moment she had stepped through the front doors. It had been such a long time since she had felt any level of safety and security.

"It's a great place to sit and think for a spell." He gave her a bright grin.

"Thanks," Kate said again then turned and headed to the doors. She glanced back to wave goodbye and saw the pastor had been joined by the blonde giant. They both smiled and waved as she left.

Walking slowly back to the store, she began to formulate an apology to Fiona in her head. Thoughts of the men at the church kept invading though. If Peter was the pastor, who was the other guy and why was he there?

Chapter 8

"Who was that?" Drew couldn't stop looking at the door through which the woman had just walked out. He didn't remember ever seeing her around town. It wasn't like Haven was big enough that locals didn't run into each other on occasion. He would have remembered running into this local.

"You know, that's funny. I never asked her name." Peter shrugged as he headed back to his office. "Why?"

"No reason." There was no way Drew was going to tell his brother why he wanted to know more. There was something captivating about her face. Something that made him want to get to know her more.

"Oh really," Peter drawled out as he nudged Drew in the side with an elbow. "No reason at all?"

"Fine. Whatever. How did your meeting with Mrs. Johnson go?" Two could play this game.

"How much did you hear?"

"Just that she doesn't want any of that new-fangled worship music or instruments playing. How are you going to break it to the worship bands we're out of a Sunday morning gig?"

"First, don't refer to it as a gig. It's worship. There's a difference. And second, start learning some hymns."

"Seriously? Look, I like hymns as much as the next guy." Peter snorted. "I do! But every Sunday? What about some more modern ones at least? Keith and Kristyn Getty have some that we could probably handle."

"I'm pretty sure Mrs. Johnson's metric for what makes an appropriate hymn is one that is at least a hundred years old."

Drew groaned. He wasn't sure he would be able to convince his worship team to play them. Maybe if they did a new arrangement. That might work.

"And no new arrangements. Play it like Gram used to when we sang them around the piano growing up."

"Come on. You're killing me here."

"Don't make me lecture you on what worship means. Again. Just do this for me. You don't have to do all hymns. I never promised that. But you need to do at least two. That was the compromise we came up with. One has to be before the sermon, and you have to end the service with one."

Drew pulled a face at his brother. "What about the band? I can play keys if I have to, but Ashley does way better. What about the other instruments?"

"I never agreed to leave them out. She might have thought I did, but I didn't."

"A little sin of omission then?" Drew laughed at his brother. "And you're the pastor! Set an example will ya'."

Peter flushed slightly. "Let me worry about it."

"Fine. I think it's a mistake though. If you want to grow this church, you need to branch out some. There are some great songs out there. You know like something by Chris Tomlin or Casting Crowns."

Peter slapped a hand on his brother's back. "I certainly do, but Mrs. Johnson and other members do not. So, for the time being we will work on slowly introducing them to other styles of worship music. I'm not going to let this be a stumbling block right now. There will be time to take it on later."

"Great. Now I need to revamp the set list for this week. Can we at least do 'In Christ Alone?' Most people don't even realize how new that one is. I think we can sneak it past Mrs. Johnson."

Drew stopped and clasped both hands under his chin. He gave his brother his puppy dog eyes. It had worked when they were kids sometimes. Maybe it would work now.

Peter laughed. "Forget it. Give it a couple of weeks and try then. For now, do some of the traditional hymns. Nate will just have to sit out on those for now. I'm sure a drum set does not meld with what Mrs. Johnson has in mind for hymns."

"Well, you can't say I didn't try. I'm going to head home and grab a shower. I'll be back in a little while to start on that list you have for me. Want me to bring anything back?"

"Naw, I'm good. See you in a bit."

The men parted ways at the back door. Drew bounded down the steps to the street and immediately began to revamp the playlist for Sunday in his mind. He'd need to get it out to the team today so they could be ready for rehearsal.

His mind drifted back to the woman who had come into the church earlier. He had noticed her the moment she'd walked through the door. She had seemed so frantic until she had stopped to see the windows.

Those windows were amazing. It was one of the things he loved most about the church. He wondered what had upset her. He wanted to go fix it. Then again, he always wanted to fix the broken ones. Maybe it was because he had once been a broken one himself until the Grants had taken him in.

What was it about today that had him thinking so much about the past? He never dwelt on it this much normally. Nothing could fix the fact that his parents had died, and he had become a ward of the state. His parents had been only children. They had been older when they'd had him, so all his grandparents were either dead or too old to care for him. There had been no one to take him in.

He began to pray. Maybe he just needed to talk with God. That always seemed to help when he was feeling troubled. It was one thing the Grants had taught him right away.

Ken and Jill had sat him down the night he had arrived to lay down the rules of the house. He had been his typical belligerent self only half listening. Most houses had the same rules anyway. Be respectful. No hitting. No yelling. Be kind. Yada, yada, yada.

Ken had got attention when he had told him the last rule. "And this is the most important rule in this house. Pray whenever you are mad. Ask God to help you calm down and see the real reason for the emotion you're feeling."

Drew's mouth had dropped open. He had always tried to hide what he was feeling, but this rule had thrown him for a loop even he couldn't hide. What kind of house was this anyway? Pray when he was mad? It was a rule he had to follow? Yeah, right, he had thought. No chance.

But he had. He still wasn't sure what had made him do it. After his parents death, he had made a promise to never believe in God again. Certainly not believe in a God that would take a ten-year-old boy's parents away from him.

It was that small thing which had helped change everything though. He had begun to pray. Tentatively at first. And it was hard to pray when you were mad. It seemed like he spent much of his waking hours praying. Then slowly he realized he was less and less angry, but it had become such a habit he continued to pray when he was feeling other things as well.

Jill and Ken had saved his life with that weird rule of theirs. One that had not only changed his entire outlook on life, but one that had made him a Grant and brought him back into a family. A family he never thought he would ever have again.

Maybe it was a good thing to remember the past, he thought as he continued ambling towards his house.

Remembering helped him be thankful for what he had instead of dwelling on what he didn't.

Chapter 9

A few days later Kate found herself once more at the stone church down the street. Pushing open the door, the familiar comfort reached out to greet her.

Fiona had forgiven Kate for her outburst. She had also kept her word and stopped pushing Kate to figure out the how and why of the necklace.

Unfortunately, the nightmares were still coming, and Kate felt herself unraveling a bit more each day. She hoped spending some time at the church would help her find the calmness she was craving.

Moving down the left side again, she picked a different window to sit next to. The plaque beneath it read "Wise and Foolish Builders." The window had four panes. One near the top showed a man laboring to build a house on what appeared to be a sand dune. The pane beside it showed a storm-tossed sky with dark clouds, rain pouring down, and the house leveled. Below were two more panes. One again showed a man laboring to build a home, but this time it was on solid ground, high above the beach and set back. The second pane showed a similar storm-tossed sky, but this time the house stood.

"Back again?"

Kate looked behind her to see the same tall blonde haired man sitting there. For such a large man, he certainly moved quietly.

"I hope you don't mind. I find it peaceful here, and I need more peace in my life these days."

"I understand. So, you like our windows?"

Kate looked again at the one she had just been studying. "They're beautiful."

"I don't think I've ever seen you around town. Are you new here?"

Kate gave a short laugh. "Not really. I've lived here for two years now. You?"

"No, I've lived here for a while as well, and I used to come here for vacation in the summer when I was a teenager."

Kate glanced over her shoulder at where he was still sitting. His hair was windblown and messy. He was dressed again in shorts, a sweatshirt, and sneakers holding a cup of coffee from the Three Cats Café.

She didn't really want to do small talk. She turned back to the window, just wanting to be alone with her thoughts. He was starting to become a distraction, a cute one, but still a distraction.

"What do you do for work?" Really, had he just asked her that? He wasn't taking her subtle hints at all.

"I own Seascapes down on the boardwalk."

"Sea what?

She turned at this. Seascapes was the heart and soul of her life. He'd better not be making fun of the name. She had worked hard on coming up with it.

She spoke slowly. "Seascapes. It's a little shop that sells sea glass jewelry, driftwood art, prints, pottery, and other things made by local artisans." She turned back to the window. That should do the trick.

"Huh, never heard of it."

Kate's mouth dropped open. Did he just say he had never heard of her store? If he had lived in town for any length of time, he would have heard of Seascapes. There was no way he had never heard of her store. She advertised all over town for crying out loud.

Hunching her shoulders, she sniffed loudly and kept her back to him. Let him think whatever he wanted about that, but she was done talking to him. How dare he insult her like that!

Drew sat in the pew chuckling at the reaction the woman was giving him. Of course, he had heard of her shop, in fact he had even gone in a time or two to pick up something for his mother or one of his sisters as a gift. He'd never seen her there though. It had always been a tall, pretty, redhead who could talk lobsterman into buying lobsters.

How had he ever missed this woman? He felt like God was playing a cruel trick on him. He had become restless, searching for someone who might become his wife.

Lucy hadn't been that person. He was more than ready to settle down and begin his own family while she just wanted to have fun. There was something about this woman in the church that had him wanting to know more about her.

Standing, he headed over to where she now stood by the windows and waited silently beside her. He wanted to see what she would do.

Kate shifted slightly to her right. What was wrong with this guy? First, he insults her store. Okay, maybe not insult, but still. And now he's standing far too close. Hadn't he ever heard of personal space?

"Hello, welcome back," a voice called from the far doorway. "Is there anything you need from me, brother?" Peter had been standing just inside the door of the sanctuary watching his brother tease this poor woman. Drew could have seen him at any point if he had bothered to look his way, but he had been fully focused on her. Peter thought it might be a good time to intervene now that they were within spitting distance. He remembered well how annoying Drew could be and he didn't want him driving the woman away.

Drew jumped. Where had Peter come from? Then he flushed slightly knowing his brother had most likely seen everything. Shoot. He was going to get grilled later he was sure.

"Nope. I'm good. I'll see you later." And with that Drew winked at the woman, turned on his heel, and walked out.

Peter watched his brother leave and then turned his attention towards the woman. Peter knew Drew was expecting a conversation later. He mentally rubbed his hands together and grinned. He was going to have fun with this one.

"Sorry about him. He sometimes can't help himself." Peter stepped near. "Do you know the story of this window?" Changing the topic, he pointed to the one she had been looking at.

Kate breathed deeply. She was still a bit unsettled after her encounter with the blonde giant, as she had dubbed him, and his abrupt departure. "Not really. Obviously, it must have something to do with building."

"Well, yes and no," Peter answered with a small grin on his face. "Yes, it's about building, but there is a bit more to the story. As the top pictures show, if you build your house on the sand and a storm comes, the foundation is ripped out. Have you ever built a sandcastle on the beach and watched helplessly when the tide came in and destroyed it?"

"Yeah, I remember doing it as a kid. I was so upset and tried hard to build walls to protect it."

"Did it work?"

"Not at all. I was almost frantic trying to save it, but in the end the tide still washed it away."

"If you build your house on solid ground, like most modern-day houses, it will stand. A storm won't hurt it. But there is a deeper meaning behind the story. The foundation we need to build our life on is God. He is the bedrock we are to stand firm on."

Uh-oh, Kate thought to herself, here we go. I knew it would only be a matter of time before he would start preaching. I guess it's the price to pay for coming to the church. No wonder they leave it unlocked. She resigned herself to listen and sat down in a nearby pew.

Peter sat in front of her and faced the windows as he continued. "Wise builders make sure their foundation is sturdy. It needs to be strong to withstand the storms. Foolish builders aren't interested in anything long-lasting. Like children building sandcastles, they just want to get it done so they can enjoy it. It doesn't matter if it lasts for any length of time."

He stopped and turned his gaze back to the window. "Feel free to stay as long as you like. I just need to go tidy things up a bit in the fellowship hall. The Ladies Auxiliary was here yesterday. They always mean well, but they tend to move things to places I can't find. It's always a treasure hunt for me after they leave."

Kate watched in disbelief as he walked away. Again, she had braced herself for a sermon, and again, he had simply told the story and walked away. He was the oddest man she had ever met.

Chapter 10

The small bell tinkled over the door and Kate looked up. She held back a groan. Agnes Johnson had just walked in like she owned the store.

Mrs. Johnson, as she had informed Kate she preferred to be called, was one of the oldest women living in their little seaside town. She had been married to the one-time mayor, so she felt she needed to be treated with some deference. It didn't matter that her husband had been mayor twenty years ago for only one term, or even that he had been dead for ten years.

She reminded Kate of the matriarch from one of her favorite TV shows, Downton Abbey. She could certainly teach Maggie Smith a few things.

"Good morning, Mrs. Johnson. How are you on this lovely day?" Kate had learned to greet her quickly, and with as much sugar in her voice as possible.

"Terrible. Simply terrible. The youth of this town have no manners. I was almost hit by a young hooligan riding a bicycle on the sidewalk. I'm simply going to have to speak with the chief of police about this matter."

"I'm sure the boy didn't mean any harm." Kate tried to soothe her before she went off on a long-winded tangent. She still was working on her never-ending to-do list. She did not have time to listen to Mrs. Johnson fret about the sanctity of pedestrian ways.

Mrs. Johnson made a noise which could only be considered a huff. "Well, I'm certain he did. Children these days simply do not have the respect for their elders they should. It would appear no one is teaching them how to behave properly."

Kate resisted the urge to roll her eyes. She was sure Mrs. Johnson would not find that proper either. Before she could again ask what she could help Mrs. Johnson with, the woman began speaking.

"Now, where is that woman you employ?"

"Fiona? She's out back working on more jewelry for our display window. Did you want to speak to her?" Kate was puzzled since Mrs. Johnson didn't usually ask for a specific employee. She would complain to whomever was in front of her at the time.

"No, no, no. Not that infernal redhead. All she seems to do is talk," Mrs. Johnson grumbled. "No, that new woman you hired. What is her name again?"

"Oh, you must mean Nancy. She's out running an errand for me. She should be back soon. Is there anything I can help you with instead?"

"She needs to be told how to be polite to customers. I was in here the other day and heard her talking to Mr. Edwards. She was downright rude to him. I would think, as an employer, you would have done a better job teaching your employees how to treat the customer. Do you not tell them how the customer is always right? She obviously could use a refresher. One would think someone of her age would have learned something like that long ago." Mrs. Johnson firmly nodded her head as she stated her edict.

Kate couldn't help but give a small sigh. Why did it have to be Mrs. Johnson who had seen the incident? It had been on a day Kate and Fiona had gone to the tide pools to look for more sea glass, the first day she had left Nancy alone in the store. She had already heard all about how Nancy had spoken to Mr. Edwards and planned to discuss it with her. Small towns weren't known for keeping secrets.

"Yes, Mrs. Johnson, I do teach my employees that very sentiment. You remember she hasn't been here long, and she's never worked in retail before. I was already planning to discuss it with her today."

"Good. Now, let's move on to your front window display. It simply will not do."

◇ ◇ ◇ ◇ ◇

Drew couldn't get the woman from the church out of his mind. What was wrong with him? He would never have treated a stranger the way he had treated her, but she became prettier and prettier the more frustrated he made her.

Just as he had predicted, Peter had come over that night with some steaks for the grill and used the same treatment on Drew. He was squirming mightily by the time his brother had finished with him. Now Drew was even more determined to figure out who the woman was.

He had thought he might stroll by Seascapes and see if she was inside. Then he might casually walk in and... And what? He'd told her he had no idea where her store was located and yet here he was, the very next day, at the store? Was it plausible? He thought he could spin it. Maybe.

His feet slowed as he saw the store up ahead. He stopped as the front door was flung open and out marched Mrs. Johnson. *Please go the other way. Please go the other way.* He was rooted to the spot. He did not want to deal with Agnes Johnson about worship music or any other issue she might have. Not now.

Thankfully, she turned away from him, sniffed loudly at whatever was annoying her this time, and marched in the other direction. Drew let out a breath he hadn't even realized he was holding.

Continuing towards the store, he peeked in through the large display windows to see who was working. The woman from church was standing at the counter talking with an older woman. From the looks on their faces, it wasn't a pleasant conversation. Drew guessed it had to be better than dealing with Mrs. Johnson and took a chance.

He pulled open the door and heard a bell jingle. Stepping inside he glanced left and right quickly, like he might be looking for something as he waited to be noticed.

"We'll finish this discussion later, Nancy. Just please, you need to be more polite to our customers. And try not to antagonize Mrs. Johnson."

"Maybe if she wasn't such an old biddy, it wouldn't be so easy."

Drew swallowed his laugh. Well, perhaps it hadn't been that serious of a conversation after all. Now he understood why Mrs. Johnson had left the store the way she had.

"Nancy, that's what I'm talking about. Respect. It goes a long way."

"Fine."

Drew turned to watch the older woman head to the back of the store. The other woman sighed and finally looked up, catching his eye.

Kate groaned inwardly. Could this day get any worse? She had already had to deal with Mrs. Johnson, then had the conversation with Nancy about Mr. Edwards and Mrs. Johnson, which did not go well, and now this. Why was he here? He had said the other day he didn't even know where her store was on the boardwalk. Had he come looking for it? For her?

Shaking her head at the thought, Kate plastered a fake smile on and asked, "May I help you?"

"Just thought I'd come check this place out. Seems a bit frou-frou for my taste."

Drew bit his lip as he watched her eyes spark. Yup. This was going to be easier than he thought. He also thought maybe he wouldn't share this particular meeting with Peter when he saw him later.

"I'll ask again. May I help you?" Kate didn't know why he was here or what he wanted, but he certainly wasn't shopping. Unless it was for a girlfriend or a wife. She felt a quick kick in her stomach at the thought. What was that all about? She didn't care if he had either, did she? She certainly wasn't looking for a relationship with him or with any other man. She didn't need that type of complication in her life.

"Hi, I'm Drew. It's nice to meet you." Drew walked the short distance towards her and stretched out a hand. He waited to see if she would rebuff it or accept it.

Kate glanced from his hand to him and back. Reaching out slowly she grasped it, "Kate." She quickly pulled away and backed up two steps.

What was that? She had felt a jolt from her fingertips to the top of her head at his touch. She flexed her fingers behind her back.

Drew swallowed before trying to speak. Well, that was something he hadn't quite expected. The electricity at her touch had stolen away any more joking he might have planned.

"It's nice to meet you, Kate. Would you like to take a walk on the beach with me?"

Where had that come from, he thought. He didn't even really know this woman. Go for a walk on the beach? Really?

"Um, well…" Kate stammered, trying to pull her thoughts together. "You see…"

"Well, hello there handsome! What's your name?" Fiona breezed in from the back room, glancing between Drew and Kate. "Did I interrupt something?"

"No, nothing," Kate quickly replied.

Drew looked at her and smiled. So, it had affected her, too.

Chapter 11

Walking to work the next morning, Kate sniffed the air. She loved the salty scent that lingered by the ocean. Gulls wheeled and screeched overhead as they made quick dashes down to the shoreline where there must be something edible. Looking out at the horizon, she watched as the sun continued to inch its way upwards. While she still wouldn't call herself a morning person, she could appreciate the beauty found at this time of day.

Approaching the store, she suddenly stopped. Propped against the door was another brown package tied with twine. It was similar in shape and size to the one she had found earlier with her mother's necklace inside.

Her breathing became shallow and her heart began to race. She knew she was close to having a full-blown panic attack. Fumbling in her coat pocket, she found her phone and hit the speed dial for Fiona.

"Morning, sunshine!" Fiona chirped on the other end when the connection had been made. "What's up?"

Kate couldn't get a word out. Black spots were floating in her vision. Taking a breath was starting to become impossible.

"Kate? You there? Are you okay?" Fiona's concerned voice seemed to be coming from miles away.

"Store. Come." Kate managed to get out between trying to breathe. Breathe in. Breathe out. Slowly. In through your nose, out through your mouth. Kate could hear Ms. William's voice calmly giving her the instructions and talking her through the exercises she had given her all those years ago to help fight the panic attacks. Just breathe. Just breathe.

Kate woke to find herself laying on the sidewalk with Fiona shaking her shoulders. "Kate! What happened? I'm calling an ambulance!" Fiona was frantic. She was trying to get Kate to sit up while also pushing her to stay down at the same time.

"Fee, stop! I'm okay. I just fainted. It's alright." Kate took a shuddering breath and could feel her heart wasn't racing like it had been. Lifting a shaking hand, she pointed. "There's another package. There, at the door."

Fiona glanced over her shoulder. "Let's get you inside." She helped Kate stand and wrapped an arm around her for support.

Kate's head was still spinning, and the back of it had begun to throb. She gingerly reached back to prod the area and winced. She had the beginnings of a large goose egg.

Fiona moved her arm to around Kate's waist and helped her walk to the door. Taking her keys from her pocket, she soon had it open and Kate settled on a stool near the front. Just like a week earlier, they stared down at the mystery package.

Taking a deep breath, Fiona grabbed a pair of scissors and cut the twine. "All right, let's see what's inside." She peeled back the brown wrappings. Once again, there was a Seascapes box nestled inside surrounded by more brown paper.

With a trembling hand, Kate removed the smaller box and lifted the lid. Inside were pieces of sea glass, lots of sea glass. They were all different shapes and colors, ranging from the more common ones to a few rarer colors such as lavender, amber, and some unique orange pieces. Kate was thankful she was sitting down.

Fiona looked at her and saw how pale her friend had become. Without saying a word, she hurried to the back room and returned with a bottle of water. She handed it to Kate and then picked up the box of sea glass.

"I don't get it. Where did this come from? Do you think it was the same person who left the necklace?"

Kate needed to find a way to stave off the second anxiety attack she could feel coming on. She didn't understand what was happening. Her head swirled with possibilities.

The last time she had seen the necklace was around her mother's neck. Her mother was dead. She certainly couldn't have sent it. And why had it been in one of her store boxes? It just didn't make sense.

And now the glass. Oh, gosh, the glass. She had vague memories of playing with sea glass as a child. It had been in a large glass container. It couldn't be the same though. It's not like it was distinctive. There was nothing to mark it as the same.

Yet, it seemed familiar. The colors. The shapes even. But she had only been a young girl. It was impossible. And the box. Why had it shown up in another of her store boxes?

As the thoughts whirled through her head about what it could all mean, she sat and focused on her breathing. Taking one last shuddering breath, she looked at Fiona with a determined look. She was done letting her past dictate her emotions. She was so tired of it.

"Just go throw it away, Fee. I don't want to see it. I just wish I knew what it all meant. I'm tired of all of this mystery."

"Kate, do you know how rare some of these colors are?" Fee had her finger inside the box pushing the glass around and even picking up some pieces to look at them more closely.

Kate wondered if she should tell Fiona a bit more about her past. Should she continue to keep it a secret or should she confide in her friend? Maybe it would help to talk it out. It might help her gain some clarity about what was going on.

Kate could still feel the panic attack hovering and knew if she didn't gain some control, she might pass out again. "Fee, I'm done with this. Let's just get on with the day. I don't have time to keep feeling this way. We need to get the store ready for the summer rush. I'm going to go in the back and work on orders." She stood abruptly, swaying for just a moment. Getting her bearings, she headed towards the back room.

As Kate entered the room, she looked up to see Nancy coming in through the back door. She was surprised to see her here this early. Normally she worked the afternoon shift which allowed Kate and Fiona to beachcomb for glass.

"You're here early, Nancy. Anything I can help you with?" Kate hoped her voice didn't betray her. She had no desire to explain to Nancy what was going on.

"No, I just thought I'd swing by on my way to the café to see if you wanted anything." Nancy tucked her keys into the pocket of her neon pink velour tracksuit. She always wore such odd clothing. It was one of the things Kate had spoken to her about on the first day, the need to dress more professionally when in the store.

"Oh, well thank you. I don't need anything though. Fee's out front if you want to check with her."

It seemed early for Nancy to be out. She had clearly stated she didn't like mornings when she was hired which is one reason she worked the afternoon shifts. Perhaps she was trying to make up for yesterday.

"Oh, no, I'll just be heading out now." Nancy did an abrupt about face and hurried back out the door.

Kate shook her head. This new employee of hers was strange to say the least. She still wasn't sure she had made the right decision when she hired her. *I guess time will tell*, she thought to herself.

Chapter 12

Drew couldn't get Kate out of his head. He had been thinking about her almost nonstop since their encounter at her store yesterday. He still couldn't figure out how had he never met her before. And why had he asked her to go for a walk with him? He was never that forward with a woman. Ever.

He continued toward the café. He hated cooking for himself and tried to avoid it at all costs. All the restaurants in town knew him by name. He was a frequent customer. He showed up at the Three Cat Café so often they knew his favorites by heart. They even made them special for him on occasion. There were definite perks to living in a small town.

He had always loved the vacations the Grants had taken here when he was growing up. Haven was a small beach town, but it grew to the size of a small metropolis in the summertime. While he enjoyed the hustle and bustle of the summer tourist season, he enjoyed the quiet winters more. There was something about winter at the ocean that spoke to his very soul.

A storm-tossed winter sea reflected what he felt whenever he thought about his parents. Not the Grants. They were a great family and he was beyond blessed to be a part of it. It was the times when he let himself think about what life would have been like if his parents had never gone out that night. What would his life have looked like now?

Drew had grown up in a small family in a small town in the middle of nowhere. Everyone had known his name. He couldn't go out to play without someone keeping an eye on him to make sure he was safe and behaving himself. That little town had been even smaller than Haven.

Then the accident happened. He had been home with a teenage babysitter the night the police had shown up. He hadn't really understood what they had told him, but then the social worker had packed an overnight bag and taken him with her. He had fought so hard it had taken two officers to wrestle him into the seatbelt.

He had cried and screamed and fought until he had exhausted himself. He had woken the next morning in a strange house, with strange people, still trying to figure out how his parents could be gone forever. They had kissed him goodbye and said they'd be back before he knew it. Now they were gone forever.

That strange home had been the first in a long string of placements. He had been determined to make all his foster families so miserable with him they would have no choice but to let him go home. It had taken a long time for him to realize there was no home to go back to.

Drew shook his head. He didn't allow these thoughts to take hold very often. He had learned it did nothing but sink him into a deep depression.

Instead he started to focus on what he had received as a result of the hand life had dealt him. He wasn't an only child anymore. He was part of a large and growing family.

Ken and Jill were amazing parents and grandparents. Now that they were older and the last of the kids were launched, they traveled around to visit each of their children and their families.

Drew thought it would be nice to introduce them to Kate. Wait. He stopped walking. What was he thinking? Why would he introduce them to Kate? That was nuts. They weren't even dating. And he knew if he introduced a woman to his parents, they had better be serious.

Smiling to himself, he let his thoughts drift towards being able to let his parents meet Kate. Maybe he needed to go back and try out that invitation again except this time he would add coffee at the Three Cat.

Whistling, he did an abrupt turn and headed towards Seascapes. No time like the present.

◊ ◊ ◊ ◊ ◊

Kate sat at her desk and stared blankly down at the pile of paperwork sitting in front of her. She couldn't seem to figure out what to work on first. Her mind was racing. The past continued to keep pushing its way in. She knew it was because of the sea glass.

She was trying hard not to remember her life after her father had taken her back from her foster family. All those lonely days and nights had been hard to bear after being part of such a large family. One weekend, when she had been around twelve years old, came to mind. She had been living with her father for almost two years by then.

Her father had been gone for a few weeks this time. He hadn't left enough money or food in the house. Weekends were long lonely days. Kate always tried to stash a bit of her free lunch from school in her bag, so she would have at least something to eat during the weekend. She had managed to smuggle a few rolls and half of a sandwich. It wasn't a lot, but it kept her stomach from constantly growling.

She was always careful not to get caught taking food. She knew if anyone found out her father was gone, they might take her away. While she didn't really want to stay with her father, she knew she might not be so lucky the next time she was placed in foster care. She could handle the neglect. She had no other choice.

She knew how lucky she had been being placed with her foster family when she had been in the system before. Their house was in high demand. They were a family who willingly opened their heart and home to any child in need. They actually loved kids and it showed in how they treated them. They weren't in it for the money like some.

On this night, her father had come stumbling home around midnight, making enough noise to wake the neighbors. Kate had quickly jumped out of bed and rolled beneath it. It wasn't until she heard him yelling back at the neighbors that she realized it was her father and not someone breaking in. They hadn't lived in the best neighborhood.

He had been drunk again. She never knew what made him return every so often. It certainly wasn't out of concern for her. She had no idea where he stayed when he wasn't at the apartment. He never felt the need to tell her.

She heard him staggering down the hall, bumping along the walls. It had been years since any photos had hung there since he constantly knocked them off, shattering the glass. Kate had begun to tire of having to sweep it up before she stepped on it in her bare feet.

There wasn't much around the apartment to even suggest a father and daughter lived there. It was stark, although very clean. Kate spent a lot of time cleaning simply to keep herself busy. There wasn't much to do in the apartment at night by herself or on the lengthy weekends.

She had curled back into bed and eventually had gone back to sleep. She knew tomorrow her father would sleep off his hangover. She hoped he had been successful in his gambling ventures and had brought home money. If he had, he would pay the bills, including the late rent, and she wouldn't have to worry about being kicked out. She didn't know what she would do if that ever happened. He certainly wasn't going to take her with him when he went, wherever that was.

The next morning her father finally rolled out of bed just before noon. He came shambling down the hall towards the kitchen. Kate was on her knees with her head inside the oven scrubbing the already gleaming surface. It wasn't like she used it often enough to get it dirty.

"Make me something to eat. I have a headache, so be quiet about it," he had growled at her.

"There's no food." Kate had quickly backed out of the oven and risen.

"What do you mean no food? Why not?"

"You didn't leave any money." Kate had answered in a soft voice without looking him in the eye. She always tried hard not to make him angry. When he was angry, he was more likely to storm out and not come back. While he hadn't hit her in a while, that was always a possibility as well. She really needed him to pay the bills and give her money to buy food.

"Good for nothing, kid!" he'd snarled, as if it were Kate's fault there was no food in the house. Her stomach had tightened as she held herself ready to run to her room to hide.

Instead of coming towards her, he'd stamped back down the hall to his bedroom. Returning to the kitchen, he'd thrust a hundred-dollar bill into her hands. "Here. Go to the store and get me something to eat. I'm starving!"

Kate doubted very much he knew what it meant to be hungry, but she had taken the money and thrown on her coat. She'd buy enough food to last her a few weeks, hopefully, especially if her father didn't stay long.

He hadn't stayed long. He had been gone the next morning, but he must have won big since he'd left enough money to cover the rent, utilities, and buy more food.

It was at this point when Kate had started taking some of the money and putting it aside for when she could leave for good. It was the start of her escape fund as she had called it. It was the only thing that had kept her going on the harder days, dreaming about being gone and never having to rely on her father, or anyone, again.

Kate had worked hard to get to where she was now. There were many times along the way when she didn't think she could keep up the pace, but she would remember how it had been living with her father and she felt a renewed sense of purpose. Her dream had been to own her own business one day and be completely independent.

Now, here she was. She was twenty-five instead of twelve. She was running her business and doing quite well. She certainly wasn't going to let her past get in the way of her dream. She wasn't going to allow her father to derail her. Not now. Not after all the hard work she had put in to get to this point. If it even was her father leaving the packages. But who else could it be?

Kate decided she needed a change of scenery. She headed to the front room. "Fee, I'm going to go for a walk to clear my head. I won't be long. Are you okay for a bit?"

Fiona walked over and hugged her. She pulled back but kept a hand on each arm and said, "Don't worry about a thing. I've got it covered. I'm going to work on making some more jewelry. Take your time."

Chapter 13

Kate headed out the door and began what was quickly becoming her daily pilgrimage to the stone church. The quiet there seemed to calm her. She didn't want to admit it, but she also looked forward to talking with the pastor who always seemed to know just what to say each time she arrived.

The man didn't fit with her idea of a religious leader. She thought he was far younger than most in that position would be. Well, at least based on what she vaguely remembered from when she was a child.

The minister at her foster family's church had been old. He had seemed ancient to Kate, although in hindsight he probably hadn't been. He had also seemed like such a giant with a loud and booming voice. She supposed anyone would seem so to a young child.

This man, however, wasn't much older than Kate. For someone so young, he certainly knew a lot about the Bible. He made it come alive to her when he shared the stories from the windows.

What about Drew? Who was he? He kept showing up at the church, too. Did he work there? Maybe he was another pastor, but she quickly dismissed that idea. There was nothing about him that screamed minister. In fact, if anything, he gave off more of a surfer vibe.

She dismissed thoughts of him quickly. She had no time for a man in her life. She refused to even consider it. Men were all alike. They just took and took and hurt people on the way to getting whatever it was they wanted. She was content being by herself. It was the safest.

Growing up in the south had not been as idyllic as one might think. At least it certainly hadn't been for her. She had always been fascinated by colder climates and had found herself relocating to the shores of Maine. That seemed like it would be far enough away from her past for a fresh start.

As she continued towards the church, she thought vaguely how Fiona would probably find the pastor good-looking. Kate wondered if he was even allowed to date. Weren't some ministers forbidden to?

Fee was incorrigible at times when it came to men. She was always pointing out different guys to Kate and constantly urging her to go on dates. Fee assured her she knew what made each one perfect. But Kate had no desire to find a man. None at all.

She just felt comforted when she came to the church. The pastor made it easy to listen and not feel judged. She knew how unusual this was for her. She didn't trust easily.

She had very few friends in her life, on purpose. In fact, if she had been given the choice, which she hadn't been, she would have rebuffed Fee's friendship. Fiona, however, hadn't allowed that. She had barged into Kate's life and, truth be told, Kate was happy about it. It was nice to have a friend, finally.

She had been turning the stories the man had told her so far over and over in her mind. She had vague recollections of many of the tales from when she had attended church with her foster family. In fact, while he was telling her about the house builders, a song had come to mind. She remembered singing it during Vacation Bible School each year.

As she walked, she began humming the tune, and for the first time in days, she found herself smiling. She had many good memories of those times. Without even thinking, she quietly began to sing the words as she continued, "The wise man built his house upon a rock, the wise man built his house upon a rock, the wise man built his house upon a rock, and the rain came tumbling down."

Her smile grew as she even remembered some of the hand motions to the song. Her favorite was when the foolish man's house went "Splat!" Then all the kids had clapped their hands together hard.

She stopped singing as she entered the church, but the smile lingered. She continued to think about what the song meant. How had he explained it? It didn't really have to do with building a house. It was how you built your life. God and his Word, the Bible, was the solid foundation and would help you stand firm while the sand or a weak foundation would cause you to fall.

She thought she understood it, but what was she supposed to do with it? Build a house? Not build sandcastles? She just wasn't sure. Maybe he would be here again today, and she could ask.

Kate headed once more for the left side of the church. There was another window there she had yet explore. She arrived at the window and read the plaque, "Ask, Seek, Knock."

She wondered what that could mean. She stood and gazed up at the window. It depicted a man in a white robe and sandals standing with only his back showing. His hand was raised to knock on a door that was partially open. Behind the door was brilliant, shining light and what looked like angels' wings.

"Hello again." Peter stepped out from the door and walked towards her.

Kate had been hoping she would see him. She turned with a slight smile on her face. It was a bit uncanny how he always knew when she arrived. She wondered if the door had some type of alarm on it that alerted him.

"I was hoping you would come back. I have been enjoying our little chats. It seems we are meant to discuss each of our beautiful windows. Do you know what this one means?"

"Not really. I was just trying to figure what on earth it meant."

"It actually has nothing to do with the earth," Peter laughed. He had been enjoying these talks about the windows with someone who seemed eager to learn. It was a refreshing change from the "Mrs. Johnsons" in his life. "This window has everything to do with heaven."

Kate thought about that statement. Heaven huh? What did a door have to do with heaven? She was even more confused now.

Peter could see the puzzlement on her face. He continued, "You see, all of us have the chance to answer the knock at the door. Jesus wants to come live in our hearts. He is standing outside knocking on the door just waiting for us to invite him in."

Finally, thought Kate, here is where he'll start to preach. Even though as a child she had been so sure she could trust Jesus and everyone else who had promised to keep her safe, it had all been a lie.

She had stopped believing in God, Jesus, and anything that reminded her of her time with her foster family. It was better not to dwell on it. It hadn't lasted. It had been obvious from almost the moment she had left that no one was going to take care of her but herself. Still, something inside had her wanting to hear what else this man might say.

"Jesus is always there, just waiting. If anyone asks him to come in, he does. Simple isn't it? He's always there, waiting and willing, but he must be asked. He doesn't just barge in and take over without an invitation. In fact, he doesn't barge in at all. He waits patiently for a request to become part of your life. On the other hand, he doesn't just come in and do nothing either. Once invited in, he will make his presence known. He will be a part of your life. It's not a decision to be taken lightly."

Kate sat listening, processing what Peter had just told her. She had once asked Jesus to do just what the man was explaining. But he hadn't kept up his end of the bargain. She had asked and she thought that meant he would always protect her. Why hadn't he done that? It just didn't make sense.

Kate looked up and smiled slightly. "Thank you for sharing the stories with me. I'll be back again soon. There are four more on the other side." She rose to leave.

Her head had begun to pound. The morning was beginning to catch up with her. Panic attacks always left a lingering headache. She feared the pain might become intense quickly. She was going to go home and rest. It had already been a very eventful day and it wasn't even noon yet.

"I look forward to seeing you again soon. You're welcome to come on a Sunday morning for service anytime. We start at ten in the morning," he called after her.

"I might just do that. Thank you." She tossed hand up to wave goodbye and continued out the door.

Kate was enjoying the visits. The calmness she felt in the church was helping her feel more stable. Maybe this Sunday she'd see if Fiona would go to a service with her.

She began meandering her way back towards the shop. She needed to talk with Fiona before she headed to her apartment. It was a beautiful day out and she hoped the fresh air might help her head. Her gaze went out over the ocean. Watching the waves come in and break on the shoreline always seemed to help her relax.

In fact, she could remember times while her father was gone when she had spent hours at the beach just sitting on the harbor wall and watching the water. It was one of the reasons she wanted to live by the ocean. It had been an important part of her life even from a young age.

She continued making her way back to the store determined not to let her past haunt her today. She was done letting her father or her mother continue to affect her peace of mind. No more.

Glancing up she saw Drew moving towards her with a grin on his face. Great, she thought to herself, just great. She couldn't even pretend she hadn't seen him and duck down the alley to enter the store from the back. And yet, she felt her stomach flip a little at the sight of him.

"So, how about that walk?"

Chapter 14

Kate had no idea what had made her agree to take the walk with Drew. Her head had been aching. She didn't have on beach shoes. She didn't want any type of relationship. Yet, she could still hear herself answering, "Sure," to his question. What had she been thinking?

Now here they were, strolling along the beach not saying a word. The long silence didn't bother her though. She had learned long ago to embrace the quiet and be okay with her own thoughts.

She snuck a glance out of the corner of her eye towards Drew. He seemed okay with the quiet as well. Usually people weren't and filled it with inane chatter. Kate disliked inane chatter.

She decided to wait and let him talk first. She was wondering how long he could go before he couldn't stand it anymore and started talking.

"Nice day, huh?"

And there it was. She flashed a brief smile. She felt like she had won some type of contest.

"It is." She didn't plan to help him with this conversation.

They continued a few more steps without speaking. "The café is just up ahead. Want to grab a cup of coffee?"

Kate glanced at her watch. She debated the wisdom of accepting his offer. A walk on the beach was one thing. The fresh air was helping to clear her head. She could justify the walk as a means to help her get rid of her headache. But coffee? That sounded too much like a date.

"Don't you drink coffee?" Drew knew how odd this whole situation was, but he didn't want it to end. He wanted to get to know this woman more. Maybe then he'd stop thinking about her all day every day.

"I drink coffee. I'm just trying to figure out if I have time. I need to get back to my store."

"Need or should?" Drew waited to see what she would say. It was hard to get to know someone who wouldn't talk more than a few words at a time.

"Should. I don't like to leave Fiona alone long."

"Don't you trust her?" Drew had her talking. Now to figure out a way to keep her going.

"Of course, I trust her. I wouldn't leave her alone if I didn't trust her. She's my best friend." *My only friend,* Kate thought, but Drew didn't need to know that fact.

"Then it sounds like we have time to walk to the café and grab some coffee. We can even pick up one for your friend. What do you say?"

Kate didn't understand why he was so eager to spend time with her. Couldn't he read the signals she was practically screaming at him that she wasn't interested? But a small voice asked why she was here in the first place if that was true.

Squashing the voice down, Kate heard herself answering, "Okay."

Drew gave himself a mental fist pump. *First coffee, then we'll see what else we can find out,* he thought. He wanted to see if he could learn more about Kate. He wanted to see if there was more beneath the surface.

The walk to the café was just as quiet as the walk on the beach had been. They grabbed three coffees to go and headed back out.

This was the least amount of talking Drew had ever had with a member of the opposite sex. Most women he had been with seemed to talk all the time. A perfect example had been his ex-girlfriend, Lucy. She had never been able to stand any quiet time.

As if his thoughts had conjured her up, Lucy was heading down the sidewalk towards Drew and Kate. He groaned under his breath. She was the last person he wanted to see at the moment.

"Well, well, well, if it isn't Drew Grant himself, in all his blonde glory. And who's this?" Lucy still had a little girl voice, which Drew had once thought adorable. Now he just found it irritating.

Lucy was glaring at Kate, as if she was the devil herself. *Shoot*, Drew thought, *this is not going to end well.*

"Lucy, this is Kate. Kate, this is Lucy. Nice to see you, Lucy, but we need to get going while the coffee is still hot."

"Whatever. And it was not nice seeing you, Drew. Not nice at all." She flipped her hair over her shoulder and yanked open the door to the café.

Kate wasn't sure what had just happened. She didn't know Lucy, but the woman had clearly hated the sight of her. "What was that all about?" She tentatively sipped from her steaming cup of coffee while she waited for Drew to answer.

"That was my ex-girlfriend. It was not an amicable breakup." Drew knew that was an understatement, but he didn't really want to talk about Lucy with Kate. He didn't really want to talk about Lucy with anyone. He knew he had dodged something when he had broken up with her. Seeing her now, he was thankful it was over.

"Let's get this coffee to Fiona before it's too cold to drink." Drew smiled at Kate as they continued back towards the store.

Chapter 15

Pushing open the back door with Drew trailing behind her, Kate walked into the storeroom and stopped dead in her tracks. Standing in front of her was her father.

All the color drained from Kate's face. "What are you doing here?"

"I'm here to see you. I'd like to talk to you. If you'll let me," he replied in a quiet voice.

"Get out of my store. Now!" Kate couldn't believe he had the audacity to show up here. She began to feel her anger rise. She wasn't a little girl anymore. He had no control over her, and she was going to make sure he knew it.

"I don't want to see you. I certainly don't want to talk to you. You have no right to be here. No right!" Her headache had returned almost instantly at the sight of her father and the pounding was increasing to such an extent that she thought she was going to be physically ill.

Drew didn't know who this man was or what his relationship was to Kate, but she wasn't having anything to do with him. "Do you need me to show him out, Kate?" He had almost a foot on the man. While he didn't want to manhandle the older guy, he would.

Kate's dad continued with his plea, "Katie, please. I've changed. I want to make amends. I want to try to fix this."

"Are you kidding me? Changed? Do you know how many times I've heard you say that to me over the years? Make amends? Fix this? You can't be serious. Get out!" By this point, Kate was beginning to feel nauseated from the pain in her head. She never thought her father would dare follow her. "And don't call me Katie. My name is Kate." She fairly seethed with rage. She was sure there were vibrations coming off her as she began to shake.

Fiona came hurrying in from the front. "Kate! Calm down. We have customers. They can hear you yelling. It's okay. I told him he could wait back here for you. He seemed to know you."

Turning on Fiona, her fury unleashed on her as well. Kate dropped her voice a few decibels, "Know him? Unfortunately, yes, I know him. Fiona, this is my father!"

Drew didn't understand the fury coming from Kate. It seemed to be out of character for her. While she'd seemed agitated at times while at the church, he had never seen her this angry. Granted, he hadn't known her long either. Maybe this was the norm for her.

And why was she so mad at her father? Drew knew there must be more behind the story. He would personally be thrilled if his father surprised him with a visit.

Now it was Fiona's turn to pale. "Kate," she gasped in horror, "I didn't know! He didn't tell me his name or who he was. He just told me he needed to speak with you about something to do with the store. I figured it would be okay if he hung out here until you got back. Oh, honey, I'm so sorry!"

Kate turned on her heel and headed back out the door she had just come through. She couldn't stay in the same room as *him!*

Drew exchanged a glance with Fiona. "Here." He thrust the coffee he had been bringing to her and turned to run after Kate.

Kate continued blindly towards the ocean, not really paying attention to where she was going, just knowing she needed to be anywhere but at the store. Her head was hurting so much now it was almost impossible to keep her eyes open. She needed to get home and lie down, take some pain reliever. She needed to get as far away from her father as she could, as quickly as she could.

"Kate! Wait up!"

Biting back a curse word, she continued walking. She didn't want to see Drew. She didn't want to see anyone. She just wanted to go lie down.

"Go away, Drew. I don't want to talk to you."

"Fine. You don't have to talk to me. How about I just walk with you for a bit? You don't have to say anything. I won't say anything. You just seem like you could use a friend."

Kate decided there was nothing she could do to get Drew to leave her alone. She physically couldn't do anything, he was much too big, but she didn't have to acknowledge him either.

It had been seven years since Kate had last seen her father. But the moment she had seen his face, it had felt like yesterday. All the pain and anger she had felt, had come crashing back. All the work she had done over the past few years to try to put it behind her, to move forward, to forget it, fell away in that one instant.

Some people seem to have parents who love and care for them, she certainly hadn't been one of those lucky ones. No, her mother had tried to kill her. She had been an attention-seeking mental case. Her father cared so little for her he spent his time gambling away what money he did earn or drinking away any profits.

He certainly hadn't cared about the nights she had been alone in their small apartment, on the wrong side of town, praying to a God she truly didn't believe existed to keep her safe. Where was he when the teenage boys would terrorize her on her walk home from school? No one had been there to keep her safe then.

It was only her own street smarts and fast feet which had kept her from irreversible harm. An occasional bruise or black eye wasn't bad considering what could have happened, almost happened on occasion, to a young girl living where she had.

It was worse when her father would come home after losing all his money. Those were the scariest times. That was when he would take his anger out on her. It didn't matter what she did or didn't do. It was never right.

Some nights she had even hidden on the streets, staying awake all night. She would stay away until he calmed down or left. It was the times she hadn't been fast enough to escape his grasp that were too hard to relive.

The happiest memories had been when she lived with her foster family. After the first few months of shyness and skittishness, on her part, she had finally seen what a loving family looked like. She always had plenty to eat and had never known a day of hunger while living there. She had clothes that fit and kept her warm. She had felt safe. For the first time in her life, she had felt cared for and loved.

For someone with such short legs, she could move quickly, Drew thought. Even with his long stride, he was having trouble keeping up with her. A glimpse of her face showed she was still not feeling well. The pinched look between her eyes made him think she had a headache.

Kate looked up and saw she had stopped at the tide pools. While she had planned to go home so she could ditch Drew at the front door, it seemed she had gone on autopilot and headed to the beach. The fresh air had dropped the pounding in her head down to a tolerable level. Out of habit, she began to slowly walk, scanning the ground with Drew trailing beside her.

Pausing at a large tide pool, she squatted down to take a closer look. It surprised her how life could survive in one of these pools until the water came in and swept it all back out to sea. Reaching in carefully, she pulled out a sea star, marveling at it. This one had four long legs and one shorter one. It had obviously lost a leg at some point. She was always amazed at how they could regenerate lost limbs.

If only it were that easy for humans, she mused as she replaced it in the water. She would love to grow a new family. One that loved her, no matter what.

Standing, she turned to look out at the horizon line. She watched the waves for some time just breathing in the salt air she always found calming.

As she began to recover from the shock of seeing her father, her headache began to slowly dissipate. There was still a slight throbbing from the fall she had earlier in the day, but the vise-like pain was gone.

"Feeling better?"

She jumped slightly. She had been so absorbed in her thoughts she had forgotten Drew was even there.

"Yes." She didn't want to encourage conversation. "Thanks, you can go now. You don't have to stay."

Taking a deep breath, she continued walking and searching. Pausing occasionally to stoop and pick up a promising piece of glass, she soon found herself absorbed in her hunt. Her mind was peacefully blank as she stopped thinking about everything but what she might make with the pieces she collected.

Drew stayed where he was and watched her walk away. He thought back to the scene at the store. There was more to Kate than she let on. She seemed like an ice princess on the outside to him, yet there was a fiery passion that had erupted at the sight of her father. It was going to be interesting finding out what she was truly like.

Chapter 16

Sunday morning arrived and Kate found herself once more heading towards the stone church. She had been able to convince Fiona to come with her, but they were meeting at the church since they lived on opposite sides of town.

She still wasn't sure this was a good idea. She had gone back to the store after Drew had left her on the beach. Just as she had thought, her father was gone. She hadn't expected him to stick around. He never did.

Fiona had been apologetic. They had talked about all the upheaval of the past few weeks between the necklace and the sea glass and now her father. It was no wonder Kate was feeling overwhelmed and stressed.

They had made plans to go to church together this morning. It wasn't something they had ever done before and Kate really wasn't sure it was a good idea now that she was almost there. What if she saw Drew? Did she want to see Drew? She wasn't sure.

Before she could figure out her thoughts, she heard Fiona calling to her. "Morning, sunshine! I've never set foot in church unless it was for a wedding or a funeral. I thought I'd wait for you. I'm getting a bit nervous about this whole thing."

"I doubt they'll try to make a convert out of you on your first visit, Fee," Kate replied with a short laugh.

"Okay, let's do this then!" Fiona exclaimed with her usual wide grin. She hooked her arm through Kate's, and they headed up the steps into the foyer together.

They shook hands with an elderly couple stationed strategically to greet everyone who came through the doors. Fiona and Kate returned welcoming replies as they collected bulletins and headed inside. Slipping into a rear pew, they shed their coats and settled in. Both heads seemed to be on swivels as they looked around taking in the entire atmosphere.

"Good morning, Church! It's a beautiful day the Lord has made, is it not? Let us stand and sing him our praises."

Kate looked up at the sound of Drew's voice. He was strumming an acoustic guitar. There was a band behind him. They were all ramping up the opening to a song.

Fiona leaned over, "Hey, isn't that the guy who came in the other day?"

Kate just nodded. Drew was a musician. She found it surprising and was interested to see if he was any good.

Drew opened his mouth and began to sing the first few lines of the song. The band were on point today and the music washed over him. He closed his eyes and sang to the Lord. He loved worshipping through music.

Kate's memories came alive during the singing. Some of the songs were vaguely familiar. She must have sung them years ago when she had lived with her foster family.

Drew opened his eyes as the last song ended. It was then he spotted Kate and her co-worker at the back of the church. She had come. He smiled at her as he slipped out of his guitar.

Kate sat up a little straighter. She hadn't realized she had been staring at Drew until he opened his eyes and shot her a quick grin. Now he was coming towards her. She glanced over as he slipped in to sit beside her.

"Hey," he whispered.

"Hey yourself," she whispered back as she felt a slight blush stain her cheeks. She fixed her gaze at the pulpit waiting for the minister to arrive.

Sure enough, the man who had been sharing stories with her over the past few weeks, stepped up to the front and once more welcomed the church and then proceeded to pray.

Kate bowed her head with the rest of the congregation but didn't close her eyes. Her thoughts kept straying back to when she had been the happiest. She had so loved living with her foster family.

Church had been a huge part of their life. She remembered going to church often. It seemed like they spent quite a bit of their week there either for a service or some other type of activity. Oh, how she missed that family. She tamped the emotions back down. Now was not the time to revisit those memories.

The sermon began before Kate had even realized it. Her gaze fell to the bulletin in her lap, and she stifled a scream but couldn't contain a startled lurch. Fiona's gaze flew to her and she whispered, "Are you okay?"

Kate nodded but couldn't tear her gaze from the bulletin. On the front, in bold black letters, was the name of the pastor, Peter Grant. Kate knew that name. Peter had been the name of one of her foster brothers.

The family had been the Grant family. It couldn't be the same person. It had to be a coincidence. Grant was a common enough name.

Her gaze flew to the front of the church where the man was now getting warmed up on his topic of God's plans for a person's life. Could it be? It had been so long, and she had been so young. She had spent more time with the girls than with the boys in the family, but wouldn't she recognize someone who had been like a brother to her?

"One of my favorite verses of the Bible is found in Jeremiah chapter twenty-nine verse eleven. Please turn there and let's all read it out loud together." There was a rustling of pages as everyone in the congregation quickly flipped to the passage. Fiona had grabbed a Bible from the back of the pew in front of them and was trying to find the verse without much success.

"There's a table of contents in the front," Kate murmured to her. Just before the pastor began reading, Fiona found the verse.

Kate could barely pay attention to what he was saying. Her foster family had lived much further south, way south. They had never come to Maine, had they? Certainly not when she lived with them. Could they have moved?

She felt Drew shift beside her. She had completely forgotten he was even there. She sneaked a quick look and he appeared to be absorbed in what the pastor was saying.

She looked to the other side and Fiona was just as attentive. She apparently was the only one who was having a hard time focusing. She looked again at the man up front and listened to what he was saying.

"Now, I'm not sure about all of you, but for me, nothing brings me more comfort than to know God has my life all planned out. Not only that, but he wants to give me a good life. Even on the days when it seems like nothing is going right, on the days when it just seems the devil has me in his sights and he's doing his best to make sure I'm miserable, the Lord has it covered. He is going to turn those horrible moments into something good. 'For I know the plans I have for you, plans to prosper you and *not to harm* you, plans to give you a hope and a future.'"

Kate thought about this for a moment. How could that be? After the life she'd had? Certainly, life was good now, but that was due to her own hard work. It wasn't because of some benevolent God who wanted to grant her every wish.

She had lost everyone who was supposed to care for her. It was obvious the Lord had completely forgotten her. It was understandable. He couldn't keep an eye on everyone. From time to time, someone must get overlooked. It was just her luck she was the one who had fallen from his view.

After all, how had her life shown any protection from harm? She had suffered plenty of harm as a child. It wasn't until she had finally broken away from her family and went out on her own that the pain had stopped.

Fiona was nudging her to stand. Kate looked around and saw the congregation had once more come to their feet and were singing a closing hymn.

She glanced over and Drew was gone. She looked around and saw him once more on the stage leading the song. She remembered it. They had sung it at the end of each service when she was a child as well.

During the final prayer, Kate couldn't help but reflect on the words they had just sung. "Praise God, from whom all blessings flow," the song had started. All blessings? Kate couldn't see many blessings in her life. At least she didn't see any she hadn't worked hard to get for herself. It just reinforced her belief that God didn't care about her, had forgotten her, or was just too busy for her.

"Kate, are you okay?" Fiona was looking at her friend with concern.

Snapping her head up, she glanced around quickly. Across the sanctuary, people were chatting, smiling, and gathering coats and Bibles. "Yes, I'm fine. So, you survived the service," Kate said with a small smile, turning the topic of conversation away from herself.

"Yes, but I don't want to talk about that right now. Why did you jump in the middle of the service like that? What happened?"

"I'm not sure. Do you see the pastor anywhere? I need to ask him something."

"Kate," Fiona said in a very exasperated voice, "What is it?"

Looking at her friend, she knew she had to tell her. Fiona didn't look in the mood to wait. "I think I may know him."

"Well, you've been coming here for a while now, of course you know him." Fiona could be sarcastic at times.

"That's not what I mean. I think…I think…" Kate couldn't seem to get her thoughts under control. How was it possible for Peter Grant, who lived in Florida, to be the pastor of a small church on the coast of Maine? Taking a deep breath, she blurted out, "I think he may be related to the foster family I used to live with."

Fiona's mouth dropped open. "What! When were you in a foster family? You never told me about that!"

"Shhhhh!" Quickly looking around to see if anyone had noticed, Kate held her hands up to her friend. "It was after my mom kind of went crazy. The state put me in a foster home with a family with the name of Grant. One of the sons was named Peter. I want to ask him. It's just that they lived in Florida, not Maine. It doesn't seem possible, but I want to ask him anyway. Will…will you come with me?"

"Of course! You couldn't keep me away!"

They made their way over to where the pastor was greeting everyone as they left the church. Kate had a tight grip on Fiona's arm. She squeezed it hard and stopped a few feet away. They watched as he finished saying good-bye to the parishioners.

"Well, hello, there," he said as he looked up and saw Kate and Fiona standing on the other side of the walk. "It was so nice to see you both this morning."

Kate moved a hesitant step forward and stopped. Her heart was pounding. This was crazy. Just thank him and walk away. He can't be the same person. She couldn't seem to move or speak. "Yes…um…hello. It was, well…" her voice trailed off. Fiona poked her in the back, clearly conveying to Kate to just spit it out.

Gathering her courage, Kate began again, "Um…I noticed your name on the cover of the bulletin. You see, well, I don't think I've actually introduced myself before. I was just wondering…does the name Kate Winters mean anything to you?"

Chapter 17

Peter's mouth fell open and he stared at Kate at a loss for words. "Kate? Katie Winters? Yes! Oh my! Wow!" He continued to stammer and stutter as his eyes brightened and a wide smile covered his face. "Social Services whisked you away so fast. My parents tried to find you. They looked for years, but no one would tell them where your father had taken you. This is amazing!"

Kate suddenly found herself engulfed in a bear hug. She held her arms stiffly at her sides. She wasn't used to random outbursts of affection. In fact, she couldn't remember the last time anyone had hugged her, including Fiona. She didn't like to be touched and Fee respected that. This man, however, didn't seem to care. Her arms slowly came up and she returned the embrace quickly before stepping back.

"Isn't God amazing? Only he could have orchestrated a reunion such as this so many miles from where we first met!" Peter continued to gush. "How are you? How's your dad? We have some catching up to do!"

Drew was putting away his guitar and saying goodbye to his bandmates when he heard Peter yell. He turned to watch him catch Kate up in a bear hug. What is going on there? He decided he didn't much like the fact that his brother was hugging Kate. Not even a little bit.

"See you guys later. Remember, we have this next week off. Ron's team is on. I'll get the music out to you soon for the week after." With a wave, he grabbed his guitar case and music and headed towards the doors.

While Kate was happy to have found Peter, she wasn't in any mood to discuss her father or what happened after she had left the Grant's house. She was still working on processing everything when she looked up and saw Drew heading their way.

"Hey, Peter, what's going on?"

"Drew! You'll never guess. Not in a million years!" Peter didn't even give his brother a chance. The words kept tumbling out of him, "This is Kate!"

Drew looked at his brother in confusion. "I know. We've met, remember." Maybe his brother had finally lost it. Maybe dealing with Mrs. Johnson was just too much for him after all.

"No, no, no." Peter laughed again. "That's not what I meant. And how did you know her name? Never mind. Do you remember mom and dad praying for Kate when we were growing up? This is Kate!"

Kate turned to look at Drew, shocked. She had no memory of him living with the Grant family when she'd lived there. Had he been there and she had just forgotten? She realized now that Peter had called him brother.

Drew's eyes flew to hers and then back to Peter's. "This is Kate? This is *that* Kate!" He wasn't sure what this meant. Did this change how he was beginning to feel about this woman? He wasn't sure. But the small seed of jealousy that had started to sprout at his brother's hug vanished.

Fiona spoke up, "It appears there may be some catching up to do. How about we do it over lunch? I'm starving!"

Kate jumped slightly. She had completely forgotten Fee. She turned slightly and pointed at Fiona. "Sorry, this is Fiona Gilliam. She's my friend and co-worker."

Fiona smiled at both men broadly as her gaze lingered a little longer on Peter. She was eager to have lunch and perhaps learn a bit more about her friend's past with the cute pastor. It was obvious there was a lot more going on than Kate had told her. She would try to find out during lunch.

"I'd love to! Let me just make sure everything is okay inside and I'll be right back." Peter smiled at Kate with his usual big grin and headed inside at a brisk walk. "Drew, want to help so I can finish faster?"

"Sure," Drew replied even though he would have preferred to stay out front with Kate.

As the men left, Kate turned to Fiona and hissed under her breath, "Don't say anything about my father. Nothing. Okay, Fee?" Kate was almost pleading.

"Kate, relax! I'm just here to enjoy lunch. I promise I won't share anything. I'll just smile and nod, okay?" Fiona still had a broad smile on her face. "Well, I may flirt a little because that pastor is cute! Do you think he's allowed to date?"

Peter and Drew were soon heading back towards them. "We're all set, ladies! How about the Three Cat Café? They always have delicious food," Peter said.

Fiona gushed, "Oh yes, I love that place. They have the best latte and scones!"

Kate rolled her eyes and then caught herself as she saw Drew glance her way and grin at her. Fiona's flare for the dramatic was in full force. She had grabbed

Peter's arm and the two of them had started down the street.

"Shall we," Drew asked as he swept an arm in the direction of his brother and Fiona.

Kate turned and began to walk. She wasn't sure what to say to him. "Hey, do you remember me?" seemed a bit much. They had been talking for the last few weeks and there had been no spark of recognition. There had been another spark though.

Kate shook her head a little. *Just ask him already*, she thought. That was the only way she'd really know, wasn't it?

She knew Peter was about five years older. She had some memories of him, but like most of those from when she had lived with the Grant family, they were hard to retrieve.

It had made surviving with her father more bearable when she had pushed them to the furthest reaches of her mind. Remembering them were simply too painful. Comparing the two lives had made the first year with her father nearly unbearable. It was a coping mechanism, which had served her well at the time.

As they seated themselves in a corner booth, Peter began. "Kate, my parents searched for you. In fact, they never really gave up. I can't wait to tell them I found you! They will be over the moon about this!"

Kate smiled shyly as she replied, "I think I'd enjoy talking to your parents again."

"What happened? Where have you been? Once your father came to get you, we never heard another thing. We were all just devastated when you left. We had kids coming and going all the time, but you had a special place in our hearts. We were heartbroken when we couldn't find out where your father moved to, especially my mom."

"It's such a coincidence we found each other here in this little town so far from Florida. How long have you been here?" Kate didn't want to feel Peter's pity about her life.

"I just arrived about two months ago. The church population here was dwindling as the congregation was getting older. When the former pastor died, I was asked to come to see if I could help bring in some younger people and facilitate it becoming a vibrant part of the community once more. It's been a struggle at times, but I love this village. I know God has a plan for me. I just need to be patient while I figure it out."

The waitress arrived and wrote down their orders for lattes, French onion soup, and cranberry and blueberry scones. As she headed to the counter to place their order, Peter faced Kate again.

"I also moved here to be closer to my brother. I think you two have met already though." Peter grinned at both Kate and Drew "You won't remember Drew though. He arrived after your time with us."

Kate felt a wave of relief go through her. Drew wasn't a foster brother. She wasn't sure why it mattered to her, but it did.

"Kate, I don't believe in coincidences. I truly believe God orchestrated our meetings at the church to talk about the windows. Today has been an answer to a longstanding prayer in our family. We've all been praying for you constantly over the years. We prayed for your safety and asked that one day we would be reunited with you. I can't thank God enough for leading us to each other." Peter finished with another face-splitting grin.

"Do you really believe that? That God brought us together?" Kate looked intently at Peter as she waited for his answer.

"Absolutely! We prayed every single night you were gone. Every night. God doesn't always answer in our timing. Sometimes it's hard to wait for Him to give us an answer, but today is an answer to prayer! Praise the Lord!"

Chapter 18

Kate knew she wasn't ready to praise God yet. She was still blown away about finding her foster brother so far from where they had lived all those years ago. Who would have thought they would find each other two thousand miles away from where they had once lived?

Peter couldn't wipe the grin off his face. "I'm so happy we found each other. I'd love to hear about your life. Would you be willing to share with me what happened after you left us?"

Taking a deep breath, Kate looked up and began to tell her story. She was surprised by her own courage. She hadn't spoken of her life to anyone other than the therapist she had seen in college. Fiona only had hints of what had happened. She was sure Peter's parents hadn't shared with him the exact reasons she was in foster care.

She glanced at Drew before she started. He had been quiet through all of this. What must he think? From what Peter had said, Drew had also been a foster child, but Peter called him brother. Had the Grants adopted him? She didn't know, but right now, she felt Peter and Fiona deserved to know some of her story.

"When I left your family, I went back with my dad, but you already know that. He had convinced the courts he had changed for the better. He stayed sober just long enough to do his home visits and court appearances. But, once he was granted custody of me again, he went back to his old ways."

Peter reached across the table and patted Kate's hand, "I'm so sorry, Kate."

She returned his smile and kept going. It felt odd to be touched. Kate typically avoided anyone touching her, but today it helped to anchor her. She felt a dose of courage, which she needed to continue.

"He moved us out of state as soon as he regained custody. We ended up in Baltimore. My father was rarely home. He would disappear for weeks at a time. It wasn't so bad when I had school, but the weekends were awful."

She glanced at Drew. He had the most serious look on his face she had seen from him so far. Usually he was smiling and happy. He looked almost menacing. What was he thinking? She shook off the thoughts and continued her story.

"When I was smaller, soon after I went to live with him, there would be days when the only meals I had were those provided by the school. There was rarely enough or any food in the apartment we had."

Fiona looked appalled. She didn't want to feel their pity, but she knew Peter would want to hear the story. She felt he deserved to hear her story since he had once been a part of it. She kept going. It was better to just get it all out now. Maybe it would help the nightmares to stop.

"I started to keep some of the money he would leave me instead of using it for rent or food. I stashed some of it to use when he was gone for long stretches of time.

"We lived in a rough neighborhood. It wasn't the safe part of the city by any means. I walked to school and back and there was a gang of boys who enjoyed tormenting me. Let's just say I learned how to fight and run fast and sometimes even that didn't save me."

Kate stopped to gather herself. Memories of the fights and the attacks she'd endured began to come flooding back. They didn't need to hear about the times when fighting hadn't saved her.

She could feel the beginnings of an anxiety attack. She started her breathing exercise. She hated how she felt. She hated the loss of control. She closed her eyes, shutting out Fiona and Peter and, most of all, Drew. She needed time to pull herself together.

Peter reached across the table and gave her hand a hard squeeze. He then began to pray out loud. Kate's eyes widened in shock, as did Fiona's. Kate quickly closed her eyes once more and bowed her head catching Fiona doing the same out of the corner of her eye.

She felt another hand grab hers and thought it was Fiona until she realized it was on her left side. Fiona was sitting on her right. She cracked an eye and Drew had reached out to take her free hand. He saw her looking and gave her a quick smile before closing his eyes.

"Lord, thank you so much for answering my family's prayers that we would one day find Kate. I can't begin to thank you enough. I know we didn't find her in our timing, but in yours. Your timing is perfect even if we can't always understand it. Please be with Kate as she continues to heal from her past. Lord, help me to help her. Let me speak your words. You are the heavenly Physician and can heal all. And Lord, please help her forgive those who have wronged her. Help her to move towards you, Father, and to become obedient to your will. In Jesus' Name, Amen."

He finished and raised his head, looking directly into Kate's eyes. He began speaking directly to her, earnestly, with no smile now on his face, "I can't even begin to tell you how sorry I am for all you went through. I know it probably seems like you were abandoned by everyone and hurt by those who were supposed to love you. I hope you will continue coming to church both on Sunday and whenever you need to during the week. I've been enjoying our window talks."

Kate nodded. She was enjoying her visits to the church as well and was glad Peter wanted them to continue. The calmness she experienced there was like nothing she'd ever felt before.

"I'd like your permission to let my parents know I found you and to share some of your story with them. I think it will help them to know some of what happened to you after you left with your dad. Would that be okay?"

Kate again nodded her head and went to reach for her water glass. She realized she was still holding Drew's hand, however. It had felt good, normal even. She dropped it quickly and continued to reach for her glass.

Taking a sip, she glanced at the man beside her. She was beginning to have feelings for him, but she hadn't known him that long. How was that even possible? He had such a look of compassion on his face. It wasn't pity. It was something else. Something she couldn't name.

She couldn't think about Drew and what she was starting to feel for him. She had too many other emotions tumbling through her right now.

She had learned years ago tears didn't help anything. She made it a point to never cry, and especially not to cry in front of anyone. She couldn't even remember the last time she had done so. "Yes, and I-I think I'd like to see them again. Do they ever come to visit?"

"I can almost guarantee you they will be here quickly once they find out about you. I'm pretty sure they'll be jumping on the first plane they can."

Kate tried hard never to think of 'what if,' but it was hard not to do so with Peter right in front of her talking about his family. That could have been her life. He could have been her brother, not just a one-time foster brother.

Then she stopped herself. If she had stayed with the Grants, Drew would also be her brother. She looked at him where he was sitting quietly. Her stomach flipped slightly as she thought about what that would mean.

"Kate, are you with us?" Fiona's voice broke through.

"Oh, sorry. What did you say?" Kate gave herself a mental shake and reminded herself it didn't matter what might have been. It was the here and now that mattered.

"I was asking when you might be coming to church this week. I'll know soon when my parents are coming." Peter's wide grin was back in place once more.

"I'll plan to come over around lunchtime in a couple of days. Does that sound okay?"

"Better than okay. I'm looking forward to our talks. We still have a few more windows to discuss," he answered.

Fiona laughed while Kate grinned at him. "I think I'd like to join you both if you don't mind? The windows are beautiful, and I'd love to hear some stories," Fiona said. While she was interested in the windows and the stories, she was actually more interested in learning about Peter. She hoped this didn't mean she was going to hell. Having a crush on a preacher seemed, well, dangerous.

"Fine with me if Kate's okay sharing the time."

"Sure, Fee. I'd love that."

Peter bit into his lunch. He chewed with a thoughtful look on his face. After swallowing he said, "I think I'm still a little shocked, but I shouldn't be. God is so good."

Kate wasn't sure what he meant, but she agreed with the shock of the discovery. She was still reeling slightly from the knowledge that she had found her foster brother so far from Florida.

"I'm so glad I found you," Peter said to Kate.

"Me too," she said and found she meant it.

Chapter 19

Drew hadn't stopped thinking about what Kate had shared with them all in the café just a few days ago. She had been a foster child of the Grants. She could have been his sister.

Shaking his head, he continued jogging. It wasn't like they were related by blood. They weren't even related through adoption. He knew he was being ridiculous about the whole thing.

He was eager to see his parents and ask them what they thought. He stopped on the sidewalk. He couldn't ask his parents that! His mom had been not so subtly hinting it was past time for him to marry and give her some grandkids. If he were to ask them if it was okay to date Kate, she would go full mom-mode on him, and they'd be married in a month or less.

He started jogging again. The thought of marrying Kate didn't seem all that bad. Sure. She had some obvious baggage from her past, but so did he. After all, he had been in quite a few foster homes before the Grants and had his own share of neglect and abuse.

Maybe, he thought, *I should take her out on a proper date before I start planning how to break it to my parents we're getting married. One step at a time there Drew, one step at a time.*

◇ ◇ ◇ ◇ ◇

Fiona walked into the back room and stopped in her tracks. Kate was sitting at her desk doing nothing. This unlikely behavior had never happened before, which is why it unnerved Fiona.

"You okay?" She crossed the room towards her friend.

Shaking her head, Kate's eyes slowly came back into focus. "Oh, sorry. I guess I was just thinking."

"About what?" Fiona settled into the chair in front of the desk. Kate had started talking more about her past over the last few days.

As Fiona had guessed, Kate began, "I was thinking about my father. There was one time when he came home and stayed longer than a few days. I think he was home for a few months. I was trying to remember how old I was when it happened. I think I was about thirteen.

"It was one of the few times he was home at Christmas. He usually left right around the start of December and I wouldn't see him again until the New

Year. It was always such a lonely time for me. It's one reason I don't care much for the holidays."

Fiona smiled sympathetically, "I never knew that. I'm so sorry, Kate."

Kate smiled back, "Once I was older, I started going to the local homeless shelter. I volunteered at the shelter quite a bit. It helped me see my situation in a better light. While I didn't have a parent around, at least I had a safe place to sleep."

Fiona loved Kate's generous spirit. She was always giving, but usually behind the scenes so that no one knew it was her. She never did it for recognition.

"It could have been so much worse. There were kids at the shelter. Little kids. They would come in with such big solemn eyes. They rarely smiled. It was just so heartbreaking."

Fiona thought that Kate's own life was just as heartbreaking but didn't say anything. She couldn't imagine how Kate had survived and turned out so, well, so normal.

Kate continued, "You could see they were in survival mode. I would try to get them to play with me in the toy area, but they wouldn't leave their mothers. They would just cling to them."

"I'm so sorry, but your life certainly wasn't a bed of roses either." Fiona couldn't keep her thoughts to herself any longer. "It's a true testament to your strength how you turned out. You know you're pretty normal, all things considered." She laughed at herself. "How did you manage to survive?"

"My father always seemed to pay the rent on time or close to on time. I've never been sure how he managed that, but he did. If he'd won big, he might pay a month or two in advance. Our utilities were often part of the rent, so I was always warm and had the lights.

"He would usually give me some cash when he came home so I could buy food. Once I was older and realized how long he could be gone, I tried to buy things that wouldn't spoil. I ate lunch at school during the week, so I was always guaranteed one meal a day."

Her nightmares had started to ease slightly now that she had started to talk about what had happened to her. It seemed sharing her secrets were helping after all.

She continued, "Thankfully the library was within walking distance. I would go there and check out books to read. I spent a lot of time reading. We didn't have a television or the internet so there wasn't much else to do during the daytime to keep busy. The streets weren't safe for me to be on, especially at night, so I made sure to be home before dark with the doors locked tight."

"I can't even imagine that type of life," Fiona interjected. "My parents…"

Kate interrupted, "Were nothing like mine." She smiled at her friend. "And that's okay. We can't choose our parents."

Kate wrapped her arms around her middle. She knew she'd had a hard childhood, but she had come out the other side a successful businesswoman. She was proud of the person she was now.

Fiona had been such a huge support over the last few weeks that Kate felt she deserved an explanation, a deeper explanation, of why Kate didn't want her father around. She had worked hard to overcome the past. She wanted it all to stay where she had placed it. Firmly behind her.

Taking a deep breath, she continued with her story, "There was the gang of boys I mentioned earlier. Those were perhaps the scariest moments of my life. I don't know how I managed to get away, but I always did. Maybe Peter was right. Maybe God was watching out for me more than I realized. At the time, I was just scared I would end up with more than cuts and bruises."

As Fiona heard more of Kate's story, her heart broke for what her friend had endured. Her father really had let her raise herself rather than staying with the Grant family. It was almost as if he was being spiteful about it. After having met Peter, it was no wonder Kate was upset about being taken from them.

As if Kate could read her mind, she said, "I was thinking of going down to the church on our way to the beach to see if Peter was free. It's a bit out of the way, but not much. I was hoping he would be able to tell us another window story."

"Absolutely! Just let me know when," Fiona replied, fully smiling for the first time since she'd sat down. The thought of seeing Peter again may have been part of that.

They began to discuss the store needs. To be ready for the summer, they needed to hire more staff, make more jewelry, and finish the contracts with the other artisans who sold goods in their store. They had only been talking for a few minutes when they heard raised voices from the front of the store.

"Uh-oh," Fiona said. "That sounds like Mrs. Johnson and she doesn't sound happy."

Kate sighed. "Let's go see what's going on." It sounded like Nancy wasn't taking what Kate had told her to heart.

Before either of them could stand, Nancy came bursting through the door into the back-office area. "That old biddy had better be gone when I get back from my break or else!" She fairly snarled at the two women as she kept moving to the door.

Fiona and Kate exchanged surprised looks. Up to this point Nancy had always been a quiet and unassuming woman. While she was a bit rough around the edges and sometimes rude to the customers, she had never lost her temper like this. But then again, Mrs. Johnson could have that effect on just about anyone.

Nancy continued past them, faster than her years would indicate. She slammed the door behind her before either of them could say a word.

"What was that all about?" Fiona looked just as shocked as Kate at the sudden departure of their employee.

"I have no idea, but I'd better get up front and check on Mrs. Johnson. She is not going to be pleased. We'll have to take a rain check on the church visit until Nancy gets back."

Fiona nodded, "Do you want me to come with you? Or should I maybe go track down Nancy and get her side of the story?"

"I'm good alone. Let Nancy cool off. Why don't you start working on orders and I'll go deal with Mrs. Johnson. We both shouldn't have to suffer."

The moment Kate walked into the front of the store, Mrs. Johnson was ready to pounce. "I don't know why you employ someone like that! I thought you had higher standards. I'm shocked at the way I was treated. Simply shocked. I expect you will finally fire that woman."

Kate sighed inwardly. Nancy had been doing better, but Mrs. Johnson knew how to press anyone's buttons. Still, she had been shocked at the rage on Nancy's face as she had stormed out. Kate would have to speak to her again about her behavior.

While Mrs. Johnson didn't purchase enough to make a difference in sales, she did like to gossip. Kate couldn't have her saying anything that might impact her store's success. Maybe Nancy wasn't going to be a good fit after all.

"I'm so sorry, Mrs. Johnson. Can you tell me what happened? I'm not sure what is going on with Nancy right now. I assure you, I will be speaking with her."

"Rude! She has no respect for her elders. You should fire her immediately!"

"That will be my decision to make, Mrs. Johnson. Now, is there anything else you would like to tell me about what happened?"

"That woman is a menace and should be dismissed directly. Since you do not care to take my advice, I will be leaving." And with that, she turned on her heel and marched out of the store, nose held high.

Chapter 20

The sound of the bell had both Kate and Fiona looking up. They were sitting in the front working on jewelry while waiting to see when, or even if, Nancy might come back.

"Do I still have a job?" While Nancy looked less like she wanted to kill someone, her voice was still full of anger.

Quickly looking at Kate, Fiona said, "Why don't I cover the front while you two go have a chat in the back?"

This was one of the few times Kate almost wished she weren't the owner. She didn't enjoy dealing with employee issues. It's why she sometimes remembered the days of running the store all by herself with joy. She was glad she'd grown enough to support a few employees, but there had been far less issues before.

"I'm not going anywhere until I know if I have a job or not." Nancy crossed her arms and firmly planted her feet as if she expected to have to fight.

"Nancy, Mrs. Johnson said you did not respect her. I'd like to hear your side of the issue. I'd also rather have this conversation in the back away from any potential customers. Please, come with me." Kate headed to the back fully expecting Nancy to follow her. While Nancy did, she was mumbling under her breath and still had the cross look on her face.

"Do you want to tell me what happened?" Kate waited. She wondered if Nancy would take responsibility for anything or just pass the blame on to Mrs. Johnson.

"She came in, like she always does, on her high horse trying to tell me what to do. It's not even her store. She needs to learn to keep her mouth shut." Nancy crossed her arms and glared at Kate.

So, passing the blame it was, Kate thought. Okay then. "You can't treat customers like that. You know this. We went over it on your very first day. We also just discussed this again not long ago after the issue with Mr. Edwards. Respect, Nancy. Remember?"

"Ha! That old biddy will get my respect when she earns it and not before."

"Enough. You can't treat customers that way. Ever. No matter what your thoughts are about their character. You will have to learn how to deal with Mrs.

Johnson in a better manner. Otherwise you won't last here long." She hated to sound so harsh, but she wasn't going to play games either.

"Are you firing me?" Nancy sounded incredulous.

"Not today unless you don't feel you can change your behavior and attitude towards Mrs. Johnson. It's up to you. What will it be?"

Kate waited and watched while Nancy obviously struggled with the decision. Kate didn't think it a difficult one to have to make, but Nancy seemed be having a problem with it.

"Fine. I'll let her have her way." And with that, Nancy marched back out to the front. Kate could hear her announcing to Fiona she was staying, and she would cover the store.

Fee came through the back door with one eyebrow raised. "Well, that was interesting. I see she's staying."

"For now," Kate replied. "It's certainly going to be an interesting summer. Ready to go? I could use a walk to clear my head."

With a nod agreeing, Fee quickly went to tell Nancy they were leaving. The two women grabbed their jackets and purses and headed out the door.

◊ ◊ ◊ ◊ ◊

"Let's run that one again. Remember tempo! Slow it down and repeat the bridge twice before heading back to the chorus."

Nate tapped out the beat on the drums to get them started and then Ashley began with the opening chords on the keys. Drew was on the acoustic guitar along with Roy on the bass.

Rehearsal had been going well. Drew was hoping to sneak this song into the middle of their set at some point. The Lord had been putting it on his heart to sing. He'd had it on his mind every morning when he woke up for the last week.

He decided it was time to listen to God no matter what Mrs. Johnson might say about it. He had been following the "two hymns" rule for a while and they would still do two hymns this week, but he had to play this one as well.

As the song wrapped up, Drew closed his eyes and breathed a prayer, "Thank you Lord, thank you, for redeeming me."

"Hey, I want to run it one more time. Do you mind? I think I could clean up that melody at the start if I had one more try," Ashley said.

"Sure. Let's do it." Drew nodded at Nate to get them started again.

Kate and Fiona could hear music coming from the church as they walked up the sidewalk towards the front doors. They glanced at each other.

"Think it's okay if we go in?" Fiona wondered aloud to Kate. "I don't want to interrupt anything."

"I don't see many cars in the parking lot. Let's peek, and if we're in the way, we'll just leave and come back tomorrow." Kate kept heading up the steps and pulled open the door.

Standing on the stage at the front of the church was Drew and his worship band. There were no other people in the sanctuary. The two women watched from the doorway.

Kate's heart caught at the lyrics Drew was singing. The song was about being redeemed and letting the past go. It talked about being free.

Fiona put an arm around her friend. Kate was transfixed by the music. She had paled and was watching the band, almost as if she were in a trance.

The song touched a part of Kate's soul that had laid dormant for so long. It was if the song was written for her and no one else. She closed her eyes and let the words wash over her.

The song ended and Drew called out, "That's a wrap everyone! Thanks for coming in early for rehearsal this week! We'll see you bright and early Sunday morning!"

He headed towards the front row where he had left his guitar case open. Movement at the back caught his eye and he looked up to see Kate and Fiona standing there.

"Hey!" He raised a hand to wave. "What did you think?" It was only then he saw how pale Kate was. He hurried toward her.

"Are you okay? What's wrong?"

"What was the name of that song? I've never heard it before?" Kate had felt a wave of, well something she couldn't quite name come over her as she had listened to the song. If she didn't know better, she would have thought it was a heavenly nudge to her soul. She shook her head slightly. That was ridiculous. It was just a song after all.

"It's called 'Redeemed' by a band named Big Daddy Weave," Drew answered.

Fiona let out a huff of laughter at the band name.

"I know. It's a strange name, but trust me, it makes sense when you realize the lead singer's last name is Weaver and he's a big dude." Drew wasn't sure what to do. It was obvious Kate was distressed, but he wasn't sure how to fix it. His instincts to make it better were kicking in.

"Is it true?"

Drew was confused. "Is what true?"

"Does God redeem us? Does he set people free?"

"He does that and more."

Chapter 21

Fiona helped Kate slip into a pew. She could see her friend was still processing the lyrics from the song. Drew had hurried off to find his brother.

The side door opened, and both Peter and Drew came striding through. "Drew said you were here. Perfect timing! I wanted to let you know I talked with our mom. She had thought I was playing a joke on her at first," he said with a laugh in his voice.

"Once she realized I was serious, she started to cry and couldn't keep talking. My father got on the phone worried something had happened to me. He was struck speechless as well!"

Kate just stared at him in disbelief. She pushed the emotions the song had brought up to the back of her mind and focused on what Peter was telling her. Why were Peter's parents so emotional about the news they had reconnected after all these years she wondered? They'd had hundreds of kids come through their home. Surely, they hadn't been able to keep track of all of them.

"They are coming out soon. They can't wait to see you!" Then, unable to help himself, he stepped forward and picked Kate up from her seat and enveloped her in a hug.

Kate was a bit more prepared this time and didn't hold herself as stiffly. Her arms even managed to come up and she returned the hug briefly just before she stepped back. "That's great, Peter. What does it mean to be redeemed?" She jumped slightly when she realized what she had blurted out.

Peter stopped and looked at her quizzically. "Redeemed? As in what God does for us?"

"I guess so. I don't know. Drew was singing a song when we got here. It was about redemption and I want to know what it means."

"It's the song I want to do soon. The one that has been in my head for a few weeks," Drew said quietly to Peter. "I think that's what upset her."

"Let's go sit by the nativity window."

The two women slipped into a pew in front of the window while Peter sat in the one in front of them and Drew behind. They were sitting not far from the one depicting the lost sheep. It was the first story Peter had shared with her.

As she had walked into the church that first day, however, she had bypassed the first window which showed the story of Christ's birth. She had a very vague recollection of the story but was a bit fuzzy on the details. She hadn't celebrated Christmas in quite a few years other than quietly exchanging a gift with Fiona.

She never made a huge deal over the holidays. After all, she had no one to share them with. The days usually consisted of her curling up on the couch watching old black and white movies or reading a book. She didn't have much time for either pastime, so enjoyed the moments when she could indulge.

"Do you remember the story of Christ's birth?"

"I remember some of it, but not all of it. I know he was born to Mary who supposedly had not ever slept with her husband, Joseph. I'm still unsure how that is even possible. There were some shepherds, three kings, and someone named Harold or something who wanted him dead."

A wide grin spread over Peter's face. "Yes, the details do seem to be a bit fuzzy. The story starts long before Mary and Joseph show up in Bethlehem looking for a place to stay."

Kate smiled to herself as she watched Peter. He enjoyed sharing his knowledge. It was evident in the grin etched on his face. He was getting into his topic as his hands began to move. He was passionate about Jesus, that much was obvious. She was simply glad she had found him. It was like finding a part of herself she thought was lost forever, a piece she hadn't even known was missing.

Drew sat so that he could see Kate's profile. She seemed transfixed while she watched his brother tell the story of how Christ had been born. A smile even played on her lips, which was much better than the pain on her face earlier.

This woman had such a broken spirit. He began to pray as he watched her, asking God to heal her heart and to open it as well. He prayed she would open her heart not only to God but also to him. He was going to pursue a relationship with her. Not only had the Lord been putting music on his heart lately, but he had been putting Kate on his heart as well.

He wasn't sure where this would go, but he knew he would have that answer before his parents arrived to question him. Not that his dad would, but his mom wouldn't even hesitate to ask if she perceived how he looked at Kate. According to Peter it was "goofy."

"What does the birth of Christ have to do with redemption?" While Kate had enjoyed the story, she wasn't sure what it had to do with her question. She had been patient, but now she needed to know. She had to know.

Fiona leaned forward slightly. She had held on Peter's every word. She was now as intrigued by the story as Kate had been and wanted to know about the connection as well.

"Christ came to earth as a baby for one reason and one reason only, to save mankind. His sole purpose was to make a way for people to once more have a relationship with God, an eternally saving relationship."

Kate looked confused. "How could a baby do that?"

"Christ was also the Son of God. He was the bridge between people and God. When he was a man, he was crucified on a cross for our sins. He took on the sins of every person who has ever lived and who will ever live. He paid the price. He redeemed us, paid for us."

Drew could see the confusion play across Kate's face. He continued to pray the Lord would help Kate understand what Peter was telling her.

His heart stopped for a moment as he realized that until she did, he couldn't fully pursue a relationship with her. It felt like someone had just dumped a bucket of ice water over him.

Chapter 22

Kate hadn't been able to get the conversation with Peter out of her head. She had been mulling over what he had told her for days. She'd even pulled up a Bible app on her phone and began reading in the Gospel of John at Peter's recommendation.

"Earth to Kate! Anyone home?"

Kate looked up. The two women were in the café enjoying a late lunch before heading to the beach. "Sorry, Fee. I was thinking about what Peter told us about redemption. I can't stop thinking about it."

"Kind of hard to believe, huh?"

And ever since that day, Drew had been scarce. She hadn't seen him much and was starting to miss him. It was weird how she had lived in Haven for years without seeing him and now she had started to miss seeing him around.

Shaking her head slightly, she returned her focus to Fiona. "I'm not sure. Anyway, what were you saying?"

"I asked if you were excited to see the Grants again."

"To be honest, I'm a little scared. What if they aren't like I remember?"

"Considering it's been a few years since you last saw them, I'm thinking everyone is going to be different. You seem to be doing okay with Peter. You'll probably be just fine with the rest of them, too. How old were you when you went to live with your father again?"

"I was ten."

"I'm sure you'll appear different to them. After all, you aren't a little girl anymore."

"I'm just worried I'm going to disappoint them somehow. It's so stupid. It really doesn't matter if they like me or not," Kate said, her voice trailing off.

Fiona looked at her incredulously. "Kate Winters! They're going to love you. You're beautiful. You're kind. You're wonderful."

Kate could feel her face beginning to turn red with embarrassment. "Okay, stop, stop! What's not to love right?" She was joking. She had never felt more unlovable.

In fact, she hadn't been truly honest with Fee. She wasn't just a little scared about meeting the Grants again, she was terrified. She had done her best over the years to put them out of her head. Remembering hurt so much. What if they rejected this adult version of the little girl they remembered?

After all, her mother hadn't loved her. At least not in a way most mothers loved their children. She had so few memories of her and almost all of them contained some type of pain.

Her father had shown over and over how much he hadn't loved her. The years with him still had lasting effects she was trying to overcome.

Fiona's voice became serious. "Kate, all those things I just said about you *are* true. You are beautiful, more beautiful than you probably even realize. You are kind to everyone you meet. Your creativity with the jewelry outshines me so much sometimes I get a little jealous. You need to believe in yourself, sweetie. You *are* incredible. I think you are even more incredible than I ever thought especially now that I know more about your past."

Kate kept her eyes focused on the table. This conversation was making her uncomfortable. She was struggling to believe what Fee was telling her. She had always struggled to see herself as Fee did. Inside she was always a scared, unloved little girl.

"I'm sure it was hard to endure what you did, but don't let it define you. You could have turned out to be a different person, but instead you are this generous, caring, amazing woman. Did I say amazing already?" At this Fiona gave a short laugh, but there was moisture glistening in her eyes.

Kate grabbed her water glass. She sipped slowly as she tried to get her emotions under control. She would not cry. She would not break down. Control. She needed to find control.

"Thanks, Fee," she said once she trusted herself to speak. "That means a lot to me."

"You're welcome, honey." Changing the topic, Fee asked, "Do you want to go to church again?"

"Sure. Maybe it will help me figure out how to act in the face of all of this. I haven't got a clue what I should be feeling, saying, or doing lately. I really hate feeling so out of control."

Just then the door opened with a tinkling of bells. Fiona, who was sitting so she could see the front spoke, "Hey, speak of the devil, it's Peter! Oops...do you think I should have said that?"

Kate smiled and turned to look. Sure enough, there was Peter standing at the front of the café scanning the seats. His eyes locked with hers and he started for their table.

"I'm so glad I found you! My parents were able to get an earlier flight. They're here!"

"Here? Now?" Kate tried to look past him as she felt the start of an anxiety attack.

"No and yes," Peter answered with a laugh. "They aren't here with me. I promise they aren't hiding outside. They thought it would better if they stayed at my place while I came to find you."

Kate breathed a little slower. She wanted this, right? She was still trying to figure out how she felt about the meeting but now it was here. She had no more time to process it.

"I went to your store first, but your employee, Nancy, right? She said you had both gone out to get something to eat." Peter had started babbling a bit and it was obvious he was excited about his parent's arrival. "Are you up to meeting them now?" He was so eager he was bouncing on his toes.

Kate exchanged a quick look with Fiona. Taking a deep breath and setting herself as if going to a battle, she said, "I guess so." Her eyes then sent a pleading look at Fiona to come with her.

Her friend smiled and said, "I'll go pay the check and be right with you. Don't leave without me."

Kate felt a little better knowing Fee was coming along. She hoped the anxiety attack wouldn't get worse. She practiced her breathing exercises quietly as she rose to leave. Her heart had sped up and she was beginning to feel a little faint. She gave herself a pep talk. She could do this. She would do this. She wasn't going to let her past continue to control her.

Peter lived in the village limits, on the opposite side of town from Kate. It was a short walk to his little cottage, not far from the church itself. While they made their way there, Kate's thoughts began to race. She continued to work on her breathing, hoping to keep the panic attack from worsening. She suddenly stopped dead in the middle of the sidewalk and burst out, "I can't. I'm sorry, Peter. I just can't meet your parents!"

Fiona stopped and grabbed one of her arms. "It's okay, Kate. Just breathe. Remember what I told you earlier? They want to meet you. It will be okay, sweetie. I'll be right there with you."

Peter had a look of concern on his face. "I promise my parents aren't scary. They've been praying for this day for years. They really want to see you."

Kate looked at him with pleading in her eyes, "What if they don't like me? What if I'm not who they want me to be? I'm not a little girl anymore. What if…" she trailed off with panting breaths. The attack was beginning to worsen.

"Oh, Kate," Peter said, embracing her. "They're going to love you. I promise."

Releasing her, he continued, "Do you remember the story I told about the lost lamb? You were the one lamb my parents had lost. For years they have worried about where you were, how you were doing, and if you were okay."

Kate closed her eyes as Peter's hands steadied her. Breathe in and out. Slow and steady. She focused on her breathing as Peter continued.

"My parents just want to see you. They'd like to talk to you and get to know you again. You were like a daughter to them. It broke their hearts when you were taken from our family. They will love you just as you are. They have no expectations at all."

Kate clung to his words. Could he be right? Could they accept her just as she was? Even with all the things that had happened to her once she left their home? It seemed impossible, but she was willing to try.

"Just give me a minute," Kate said. She kept up her deep breathing for a bit longer and worked at calming her racing thoughts. Taking one more deep breath, she said, "Okay, I'm okay. Let's go."

Chapter 23

Peter called out as he led the two women in through his front door, "Mom? Dad? We're here!"

Peter stepped aside to let Fiona and Kate enter after him. His parents, Ken and Jill Grant, stood in the middle of the living room with their eyes glued to the doorway.

It was apparent in one quick look, that Peter had inherited his father's build. Ken was an older version of Peter, just greyer. He sported a goatee as well that had a more gray than brown in it.

Jill was only slightly shorter than Ken. Her hair had gone white and she wore it in a short bob. She was a slender woman who was aging well. She looked much younger than her years.

Jill's hands flew to her mouth. Her eyes locked with Kate's. Kate couldn't figure out how Jill knew her, but it appeared there was no question as to which of the women walking into her son's house was the one who had once been her foster daughter.

Kate found herself engulfed in not one but two sets of arms at the same time. Her own arms slowly came up around them. Oddly, she didn't feel the urge to pull away. Instead, she found herself leaning into the hugs. They even felt familiar.

"Oh, my sweet Katie. We couldn't believe it when Peter told us he had found you. Here! In Haven, no less," Jill began. Stepping back, she had to stop and gather herself.

Kate swallowed hard as she saw the emotions on Jill and Ken's faces. She realized where Peter had inherited his wide grin. There was a similar one stretching across Jill's face as she stared at Kate.

She continued, smiling and crying all at the same time, "God is so good! We finally have an answer to our prayers! It's been so long in coming and it's been so hard to wait for the answer. I can't... I just..." Her voice trailed off as she succumbed to the sobs she had been trying to hold back. She tugged Kate back into another embrace and held on tightly.

Kate closed her eyes. She was feeling emotions she hadn't felt in years. She swallowed hard in order to keep hers in check. Jill pulled back again and cradled Kate's face in her hands. She stared at her, drinking in all the changes, as she smiled through her tears.

Kate felt another pull on her arm as she was turned around and enveloped in a strong masculine hug. This time it was Ken drawing her close. He was no longer content to wait or share her with his wife.

He spoke into the top of her head tucked under his chin, "Katie, I am thankful the Lord has returned you to us. I have spent so many sleepless nights praying for you. I would be sound asleep, and suddenly wake up with thoughts of you on my mind. I always knew it was the Lord speaking to me, telling me to pray for you right then. I would sometimes wake up Jill and often I would just lay there and pray for your safety. Other times I would have a strong feeling to pray for you during the daytime as well. The Lord always seemed to know when to nudge me, to let me know you needed some heavenly help."

Ken had prayed for her? Kate couldn't understand this. Her mind was spinning as she tried to reason it out. Why would he have prayed for her? It didn't make sense. There was no way he could have known when she was in trouble, was there?

Ken pulled back and stared at her just as his wife had done moments before. Kate squirmed a bit under the scrutiny. Did he find her wanting? Would he change his mind? Kate couldn't fathom why they wouldn't have just forgotten about her. Why would they have continued searching and praying for her? They had so many other kids coming through their doors. What made her so memorable?

Kate shot a quick glance to where Fiona was standing off to the side. Fee had both hands over her mouth and tears were coursing down her friend's face. At this, Ken pulled her once more into a tight embrace.

Peter cleared his throat, "Um, Dad, do you want to let her come up for air there? Maybe we could all sit on the couch and talk?"

Breaking away, Ken heartily laughed. "Of course! First, I think we should all give thanks to the Lord for this day. Our Katie has been returned to us. What a blessed day this is!"

Jill and Ken sat together on the couch. Peter and Fiona sat in the two wingback chairs off to the side. This left the large ottoman in front of the couch for Kate to sit on.

As soon as everyone was settled, Ken began to thank God, "Dear Heavenly Father, we come to you today with great thanksgiving. We cannot even begin to express our thanks to you for returning Katie to not only our embraces, but to our family as well. We have spent many years asking for this to happen. In your perfect timing, you have done as we asked. Lord, help us as we become reacquainted. Give us help as we heal and reestablish our relationship. Thank you, Lord, for being so good to us. In Jesus' name, Amen."

Lifting her head, Kate looked at where the Grants were sitting side by side on the sofa. She knew she should say something but couldn't quite figure out what. She didn't want to talk about her life with her father but knew she couldn't avoid it. They would want to know. She was still trying to understand how they could have continued looking for her! Who does that? She was just a foster kid. Why would they care what happened to her once she left their house?

Jill began to speak, "Katie, I know this must be hard for you. And I know we haven't seen each other in so long, but know this, we never, ever stopped thinking about you. It broke our hearts when your caseworker arrived to take you away. Even though we knew they had found your father, we had always thought of you as our daughter. Letting you go was the most painful thing we ever had to do.

Kate swallowed hard. She was still struggling with the fact that the Grants were here, in front of her. Memories were rushing in from her time with them.

Good memories. Memories of laughing and playing. Memories of when she felt safe.

"When you arrived, you were such a quiet and sick little girl. We needed time to nurse you back to health. You were such a fighter. Soon you were enmeshed in our lives and it was almost like you had always been there. I thought of you as my daughter after only the first two months. In fact, within that time you even started to call me 'Mama.' I was so glad God had blessed us with you."

As Jill spoke, Kate continued to remember. They had always been there, the memories of living with the Grants. She had called Jill "Mama" and Ken "Papa." The memories kept flooding back.

Kate began to do her deep breathing exercises once more and feared she was on the verge of losing it. She didn't want to lose control right now. She wanted to learn more about what had happened before she'd left. Maybe it would help her put her past behind her finally. She was tired of the control it seemed to continue to have on her emotions and her life.

Jill continued, "You had been with us so long, years instead of months. That was quite unusual for us at the time. They had given up looking for your father and the court had deemed your mother unfit to care for you. We began praying about the possibility of adopting you and we let your caseworker know. We wanted the state to know you had found a forever home if they would allow us to keep you."

Kate looked across at where Fiona and Peter were sitting. What did they think of this story? Fiona had always had such a stable life and so had Peter. They both had parents who had loved them. Kate felt a stab of jealousy as a small "what if" tried to take root. She pushed it aside.

Life hadn't given her a happily ever after. She wasn't a Grant and never would be. She couldn't dwell on that though. She knew if she started to focus on what might have been, she might lose control. It was why she hadn't focused on the memories of life with the Grants. She returned her attention to Jill as she continued with the story.

"When you were nine, we found out your mother had died of an accidental overdose while in the state hospital. It seemed it was the time to begin pursuing our plans for making you our child, so we began the application process to adopt you."

Kate broke in, "How come I didn't know any of this? This is the first time I've heard how my mother died. My father always told me it was my fault." She broke off and swallowed a sob trying to rise in her throat. She refused to cry.

"Kate, it was never your fault. You were only a child. We never said anything because we didn't want to burden you with any of this when you lived with us. We would have told you one day if you had stayed. You had the right to know."

Kate allowed the words to sink in for a moment. Was it true? Could she believe it? She wasn't sure. She had lived with the lie so long that it felt like it was true. "What about my father?"

Jill continued, "Halfway through the process we found out the state was making a new attempt to find him. In all the years you lived with us, he never contacted them. I'm not sure he even knew where you were until he heard from your caseworker."

"Or he just didn't care," Kate muttered.

"I think he did, honey. In his own way. Within just a few months, he was there. We were so close to finalizing everything when he came forward to tell the court he wanted to be your father again. He wanted to raise you himself. He wasn't willing to give up his parental rights."

Jill began to tear up at this point. Her husband picked up the story where she had left off, "We fought to keep you, Katie. I think it's important you know that. We petitioned the court. Your caseworker worked hard for us as well. We feared if you went back to him, he wouldn't take care of you properly. The court seemed to take forever to finally reach a decision."

He heaved a great sigh of distress and his face seemed to crumble a bit as he continued, "Our hearts broke into a thousand pieces the day we found out the court had ruled against us and you were being given back to your father. He had been going to various twelve step programs for six months. He had sponsors who testified he was following the programs and staying sober. He even had a job. His employer said he had been an exemplary employee."

Kate knew she had gone pale. She had been ten years old when she was taken from the Grants and placed back with her father. How different her life would have been had the court ruled against him.

Fee leaned towards her friend. "Are you okay? Do you need anything?"

Taking a gulping breath, Kate looked at Peter, "I need a minute. Can I use your bathroom?"

"Sure, it's right down the hall. Second door on the right." He pointed the way.

Everyone watched as Kate escaped the room.

Chapter 24

Drew knew his parents were in town. Peter had called him last night to let him know. He also had told Drew they were going to meet with Kate today. He prayed as he walked that the meeting was going okay.

He had been praying even more lately than normal. Every time he found himself concerned with how Kate would react to his parents, he prayed. Every time he started to dwell on what life had been like before he had lived with the Grants, he prayed. He was praying a lot.

The café was just up ahead. He was taking a break from a job he was working on nearby. Victoria Rivers, a new mom, had hired him to put shelves up in her laundry room. He was looking forward to a pastry, coffee, and maybe some conversation. Anything to take his mind off Kate. He had been avoiding her lately and he knew it.

Until she decided to make a commitment to the Lord, he couldn't make a commitment to her. He was wrestling with the Lord about it right now. Why would God have brought her into his life if he didn't want more for them?

His mind was still on his problem as he pushed open the door to the café. He muttered under his breath when he saw Lucy sitting at a table alone. As he was trying to decide how much he needed the coffee and baked good, Lucy looked up and spotted him.

"Drew!" Lucy rose and rushed over to where he was standing. "How are you? I've missed you. Why don't you come sit with me? We can talk."

Drew tried not to wince at her voice. How had he ever thought it adorable? It made her sound like a little girl. Looking back on his time with her, he also saw how she had acted like a little girl.

"Thanks, but I have to get back to work. I'm just here to grab a quick snack and some coffee. I can't stay."

Lucy poked her bottom lip out in an exaggerated pout. "Oh, come on. Just a few minutes. You know you want to."

She actually batted her eyes at him. He couldn't believe it. She always hated being told no. Nothing used to irk her more. Now he didn't care about annoying her.

"I said no, Lucy. I'll catch you later." Drew strode up to the counter and placed his order, forcing himself not to look back over his shoulder to see how well his refusal had gone over. He knew it wouldn't be good.

One of the three sisters who ran the Three Cat Café handed him his donut and coffee without saying a word but did give him one raised eyebrow. He shrugged his shoulders as he placed the money on the counter with a nod of thanks and turned on his heel to leave. Haven was too small of a town for everyone not to know the situation between Lucy and himself.

Sure enough, Lucy was still standing where he had left her. If looks could kill, he wouldn't have been able to take another step. Since they didn't, he continued on his way and added a prayer up to God asking that his ex-girlfriend would start leaving him alone.

◊ ◊ ◊ ◊ ◊

Kate looked at herself in the mirror. Staring at her reflection, she thought about her past. Why had she come today? Wouldn't it have been better to never know? To just always think the Grants hadn't wanted to keep her?

Running water, she splashed some on her face. The coolness eased the heat and helped with the pain in her eyes. She was tempted to rummage through Peter's medicine cabinet to see if he had a mild pain reliever. Her head had begun to pound.

There was a tap on the door, and she heard Fiona's voice. "Anything I can do, Kate?"

Kate walked to the door and cracked it open enough to see her friend. "I'm okay. I could use a drink and some Tylenol or something though. My head is killing me."

Fee slipped inside and shut the door behind her. "I snagged my purse before coming to check on you. I think I have something. Let me look."

Fiona began pawing through her bag. She found a small bottle of tablets and shook out two into Kate's hand. Not seeing a cup, she swallowed the pills and used her hand to scoop some water into her mouth.

"Thanks. Think I can hide out until they all leave?" She gave Fiona a shaky smile. "I guess that won't work since they are all staying here, huh?"

Fiona hugged Kate quickly. "It's going to be okay. It's obvious they love you. But what do you want to do? Do you want to stay some more or go home? I can get you out of here, no problem. Just say the word."

Kate knew Fiona would do whatever she asked. She would run interference for her if needed. She just wasn't sure what she wanted. While Ken and Jill seemed great, she was beginning to feel overwhelmed by all the emotions facing the past was bringing up.

"I think I want to go home for now. I need a break to process what they've told me so far."

"I'm on it. Just follow me," Fee said as she grabbed Kate's hand and headed back to the living room.

Three heads snapped up as the two women entered. Kate could see that Jill had been crying again and it looked like Ken was watery eyed as well. She didn't want to hurt them, but she didn't think she could stand to listen to more right now. She always believed no one really wanted her. To learn there was a family who did was breaking her heart and she swore she'd never let that happen again.

"We've got to get back to the store. We have a shipment coming in that we need to be there to sign for. Um, both of us," Fee said with a straight face.

Kate knew she was trying her best, but she wasn't a great liar. That was one thing Kate loved about her friend. She never wondered about what Fee intended when she said something, she always said exactly what she meant.

Jill's head snapped up. "Are you sure you don't want to stay a little longer? We'd love to talk some more and see what you've been up to. Peter told us about your store. We thought we could walk over with you after."

Kate squeezed Fee's hand and then let go. She knew Fiona would understand what she was asking of her. Better to have Fee do it, she thought. Maybe they'd believe it more. Maybe.

"Um, well, you see, we have a lot of inventory to do and things to get up on the shelves. Now isn't a great time for a tour." Fiona was starting to blush, which was the telltale sign she was fibbing.

Kate shot a look at Fiona and then turned to the room. "I'm sorry, I just need some time to process what you've told me so far. Please understand, but I just really need to go now."

With that, Kate headed to the door. She couldn't stand there anymore and watch Fiona flounder and feel like she had to stay and talk. She needed to get some fresh air to clear her head. Did what they shared change things? She wasn't sure, but she knew she needed to leave and leave now.

"So, yeah, what she said," Fiona trailed off as she quickly followed Kate.

Peter joined his mother and father who were all now standing. "How about we come by the store tomorrow? We could come by at lunchtime and go to the café afterward."

"I'll let you know," Kate said as she shrugged into her jacket. Pulling open the door she looked back, "I know this sounds trite but it's not you, it's me."

She kept walking out the door and hoped Fiona was right behind her. She didn't stop to check but continued moving down the sidewalk. Her foster parents had loved her. They had wanted to keep her. What was she going to do with that information?

Chapter 25

Kate had spent the night going over what the Grants had told her yesterday. She still wasn't quite sure she believed them. No one had ever wanted her. Her own mother had tried to kill her on multiple occasions. It was obvious she hadn't wanted Kate. Her father had disappeared and reappeared in her life, just like he was trying to do now, more times than she could count.

She hurried down the sidewalk towards her store. She had overslept this morning. After tossing and turning all night, she had shut off her alarm and went back to sleep by mistake. She couldn't remember the last time she had done that. As a result, she was now thirty minutes behind her usual time. Kate hated being late.

As she rounded the corner of the block to her store, she slowed in her tracks. She knew it was silly, but she hadn't been using the front door like she typically did. Not since the two jewelry boxes had shown up. She had started using the back door. So far, there hadn't been any more unexpected deliveries.

This morning, however, there was definitely something at the store that shouldn't be there. She hurried down the alley to the back entrance.

A gasp escaped and she clapped a hand over her mouth. Someone had spray painted her store. Red marred her shop everywhere with words like "liar" and "get out!" covering the walls and the back door.

She ran around to the front of the building to see if they had spray painted the front in a similar manner. There was no extra color, but she held back another gasp. They hadn't spray painted the front, but they had tossed a large rock through one of the display windows.

Looking closely, she could see they had painted a word she hadn't heard since she had been walking home alone on the streets of Baltimore. She fumbled in her bag to call… She stopped. To call who? Fiona wouldn't be of any help. She should probably call the police.

She began to press the numbers, but before she could hit send, she heard a voice behind her. "Man, what happened here?"

She whirled around to see Drew standing on the sidewalk, sides panting. He must have been jogging, she thought. She drank in the sight of him as well. His hair was tousled from the wind. He looked good. She realized just how much she had missed seeing him.

"Someone spray painted the back of the building and tossed a rock through my front window for good measure. I was just getting ready to call the police to report it."

"Anything I can help with?" Drew heard himself asking. He did a quick look at Kate, up and down. She seemed to be holding up well considering the circumstances. Although, he supposed it could be worse.

"Do you know how to remove spray paint?" She asked wryly as she completed her phone call and answered the 911 operator on the other end.

Drew walked around to the back of the building to check out the damage while Kate trailed behind him still talking to the police dispatcher. He stopped and looked at the words left behind. Someone had been seriously irked at Kate. It was obvious this wasn't a random act of vandalism. The words were specific and vicious.

Kate ended the call and turned to Drew. "So, what do you think? Is there an easy way to get this off?"

Kate waited for Drew to answer and realized she wasn't as upset by what happened as she normally would be. As she tried to figure out why, she looked up and met Drew's gaze. She felt comforted instantly. Could it be Drew's presence? Was that what was helping her not to become anxious? She shook off her thoughts of Drew and moved her gaze back to the store.

Drew willed his heart to slow as he also tried to remember to breathe. He wanted nothing more than to pull Kate into his arms and tell her he would not only help her today, but he'd always be there for her. *Stop it, Grant*, he told himself.

He cleared his throat and replied, "I have a power washer. I'll run home and get it. That should work to get most of it off."

Before Kate could even thank him or agree to the help, Drew spun on his heel and started running towards home. The extra jog should help clear his head, he thought.

He heard Kate yell after him, "Maybe you should drive back!"

He grinned as he tossed a hand up to acknowledge her comment. He began to pray again for God to intervene in Kate's life and soon.

Chapter 26

Kate had enjoyed working with Drew cleaning up the store. He ended up being more help than she realized she had needed, especially with the front window. He'd had a replacement ordered and installed, with Peter's help, within just a few days.

She had called Fiona just after Drew had left to get the power washer and she had shown up in her characteristic whirlwind. She had been angry and demanded to know what the police were going to do about catching the "miscreant."

Kate had laughed at her. "Miscreant, huh?"

"Well, what else are they! What was the point of this? I don't get it. First, the necklace. Then the box of sea glass and now this! You are not having a good spring. You know that, right?"

"Gee, thanks for the recap."

Kate had been glad Drew had returned in his truck with the power washer at that point. An officer had shown up around the same time to take a statement and get photos before anything was cleaned up.

He had told Kate he would see about getting footage from any area security cameras to see if they could find the culprit. He hadn't appeared very hopeful.

Now it was as if nothing had happened. Fiona had helped redo the display in the broken window area. It had taken a day or two just to empty it all and vacuum up all the shattered glass. Thankfully, none of the merchandise in that window had been stolen or damaged beyond repair.

She had been surprised when Peter, Jill, and Ken had shown up shortly after Drew to help with the cleanup. "It's what family does," Jill had said as she had taken the shop vac out of Peter's car.

Drew had just smiled and said, "I called them. I thought you could use the help."

Kate had been overwhelmed standing there seeing everyone pitching in to help clean everything up. She'd always relied on herself. Now she had a family, if she wanted it she guessed, who would be willing to do anything to help her.

She had been glad Ken and Jill hadn't said more about the time she had been with them as a child. The past had been too prominent in her life lately. It was time to put it aside and look towards what the future might hold. She was ready to move forward.

Kate threw off the thoughts of the last few days as Fiona moved back from the display they had been working on. Kate liked to change things up weekly so there was always something new to see in the windows.

Kate stepped back to get a different view of the display. "What do you think?"

Fiona dusted her hands to signify it was complete. "I think it's perfect. I also think it's time to take a break. Let's go to the café for lunch. My treat."

"Sounds great. Let me just grab my purse from the back. I'll let Nancy know we're heading out. It sounds like she just got here."

"I'm coming. I need to grab my bag, too."

The two women chattered companionably as they headed into the back of the store. Kate was the first through the door and she stopped short causing Fee to bump into her from behind and push her further into the back room.

The person standing just inside the back door wasn't Nancy. It was her father. Why was he still in town? Didn't he get that she didn't want to see him? Now or ever!

"How did you get in here?" Kate asked in a steely voice. "I told you to leave. I don't want to see you. Get out. Now."

"The door was unlocked. Katie, honey, I just wanted…"

"Do not ever call me honey. Ever. And my name is Kate in case you've forgotten. Now leave."

"I'm sorry. Kate. If I could change the past, I would. I just need to know you've forgiven me. I'm a changed man. Trust me."

"Trust you? Are you kidding me? Like I trusted you to protect me in that neighborhood we lived in. Like I trusted you to keep me safe. You mean like that?"

"I know I can't make up for what I did, Kate, but I'd like to move forward if we could. I'd like to get to know you."

"You had your chance. You blew it. Now leave before I call the police and have you arrested for trespassing." Kate could feel herself getting more and more upset. She was not going to have a panic attack right now. She simply wasn't going to allow her body to go there. She would stay in control. She would.

"What can I do to make it up to you? I'll do anything. Anything you say."

"There is nothing you can ever do to make up for what you did to me as a child. You can't make up for the nights I was all alone in our apartment hoping no one broke in. You can't make up for the days I had to walk home alone and pray no one attacked me. Did you ever once wonder where the black eyes and bruises came from? Did you even care?" Kate's voice broke. She stood tall and faced him. He no longer had any power to hurt her. "Leave. Just leave. Now."

She watched as her father hung his head and began to walk away. At the door he turned back.

"I know I can't change the past, Kate. I know I can't do that. But I can say again, I'm so sorry I failed you. I never meant to do that. I never meant to become the man I did."

With that he continued out the door, closing it gently behind him. Kate breathed deeply to steady herself. She counted to ten and then did it again. She was not going to let this moment destroy her or define her. She was stronger than this. She was.

"Are you okay?" Fee asked as she reached out a hand to grasp Kate's hand. "Can I get you anything?"

Kate just shook her head. Her quiet, orderly life had been anything but over the last few weeks. Why was all of this happening now? She just couldn't understand it all. The control she craved was unraveling around her.

"It's going to be okay, honey. I promise."

"Don't make promises like that, Fee. It hasn't been okay for a while now."

Before Fiona could respond, the door banged open.

"I said get out!" Kate yelled by reflex, assuming it was her father coming back to try again.

Except it wasn't her father, it was Nancy finally showing up for her shift. "Fine! But that's not very professional, is it now?"

Kate shook her head. "No, I'm sorry. I thought you were someone else."

"So, you're not firing me?"

"No, I'm not firing you, Nancy. Someone was just here, and I had told him to leave. I thought he had come back."

"Who was it?"

"It doesn't matter. Fiona and I are going out to lunch. You're in charge of the store. We'll be back in an hour or so."

With that, Fee and Kate grabbed their bags and headed out the door.

Chapter 27

Drew whistled as he headed towards the café. He was meeting his parents and Peter there for lunch. He thought back to how much he had enjoyed helping Kate fix up her store.

He was puzzled by who would have defaced it like that. From what he knew of Kate so far, she was quiet and shy and didn't have any enemies. But from some of the words plastered on the sides of the store, someone did not care for her very much at all.

He turned the corner and stopped. What was she doing there? Lucy was sitting on the sea wall just outside the pharmacy which was next door to the café.

Sighing, he continued forward. He didn't have time to duck down the alley and go around. He was already running late and one thing his mother disliked was tardiness. She had drilled into their heads when they were younger, "It's just rude. Be a good steward of other people's time. Be prompt."

"Drew! Well, what a surprise. I was just sitting here enjoying the view."

Drew suspected she had seen Peter going into the café and she was waiting to see if he would show up. "Hi, Lucy. Got to run."

"Where to? Off to see your girlfriend?" Lucy's usually pretty face now had a sneer of disgust on it.

Drew stopped and looked at the woman he had once dated. "I don't have a girlfriend, Lucy. I'm not seeing anyone."

"Right. Like I believe that. I've seen you two walking together, having coffee together. I'm not stupid. Is that why you broke up with me?"

Drew quickly thought back over the last few weeks. Kate. She must mean Kate. Was she stalking him? How else would she have known they had been spending time together otherwise?

"I'll repeat it one more time, Lucy. I am *not* dating anyone. Stop stalking me and leave me alone."

"Fine. If you aren't dating her, then why is she walking up the sidewalk right now. Tell me that!"

He turned to look and sure enough, Kate and Fiona were headed their way. Fiona lifted a hand and waved to him as she leaned over to say something to Kate.

His eyes darted toward Kate and he caught the slight flush that stained her cheeks. Before he realized what was happening, he felt a shove as Lucy ran past him.

"I'll teach you a lesson! Keep your hands off my boyfriend!"

He whirled to see Lucy running headfirst at Kate. Kate dropped her purse and used her hands to push Lucy, using the woman's own momentum to deflect her.

Lucy stumbled to her knees. She jumped back to her feet and, with a shriek of rage, came at Kate again. Once more Kate simply pushed Lucy aside.

Lucy gained her feet again. She seemed to be taking a moment to figure out her next plan of attack.

"What is your problem?" Kate yelled at her.

"You! You're my problem. You can't have him! He's mine!" Lucy again came at her for a third time.

A small crowd had gathered to watch the two women. Drew couldn't decide if he should wade in to help or not. Kate had been doing well holding her own up to this point.

This time, as Lucy lurched forward to attack her, Kate stepped forward and popped a closed fist into the other woman's face. Lucy dropped to the ground with her hands to her nose as blood began to drip.

"Look. I don't know who you are or what you're talking about but leave me alone. Got it?"

"You broke my nose! You broke it! I'm pressing charges! You'll pay for this!"

Drew felt it was time to come forward. He stepped close to Lucy and stooped down, so he was at eye level with her. "Lucy, every person here is going to say how you attacked Kate first. She was only defending herself. Now, let it go. Leave me alone or I'll be the one pressing charges."

Drew walked towards where Kate and Fee were standing. He had a grin on his face. "So, where did you learn how to do that?"

She looked less than amused, "On the streets of Baltimore. Who is she?"

"My ex-girlfriend. She's been having a hard time coming to terms with the 'ex-' part of that word."

"Fine. Now, if you'll excuse us, we're heading in for lunch."

Kate brushed past Drew as she grabbed Fee's arm to haul her along with her. He might think it funny she had just hit his ex-girlfriend, but Kate thought it anything but.

Fee looked at Kate but kept her mouth shut. She also tried to hide the smile on her face. She remembered Kate saying she had been in fights when she was growing up, but she hadn't really considered that Kate would have learned to be a fighter.

"Nice punching, Rocky."

"Shut up, Fee." But there was a grin curling at the sides of Kate's mouth as she said it.

Drew watched the two women walk away and enter the café. He wondered if Kate knew his parents were inside waiting for him. He wasn't sure how he was going to explain this to mom. Well, he might as well face the music now. It certainly wasn't going to get any easier the longer he stayed outside making himself even later.

Turning to follow Kate and Fiona he heard Lucy call his name. "Drew! Wait! Don't go. Please."

He glanced over his shoulder at her. "It's over, Lucy. Get it through your head. I'm done. We're done. There is no us."

He hadn't wanted to be so harsh on the heels of her fight with Kate, but it had gotten out of hand. She somehow believed he was dating Kate. While he wanted to, he wasn't. And Lucy's actions had brought Kate into their issues. No more.

He kept walking as she continued to call after him. He pulled the door open and let it shut behind him, blocking out Lucy's voice. Scanning the restaurant, he spotted his parents and Peter and it looked like they had invited Kate and Fiona to join them. Well, this would be an interesting lunch. He chuckled a little to himself as he moved towards the table.

Kate hadn't wanted to sit with the Grants today. She didn't want to hear any more about how they had wanted to keep her. She especially didn't want to hear it so close on the heels of dealing with her father and the fight with Drew's ex-girlfriend just now.

"We'd love to have you both join us," Peter had offered. Even though she had enjoyed getting to know everyone better as they had helped clean up the store, she wasn't ready for more today. She just wanted a quiet lunch with her friend.

Feeling like she couldn't refuse, Kate had nodded and slid into the booth beside Peter. That left Fee to slide in beside Jill. She wasn't sure if sitting beside her former foster mother would have been better than sitting across from her, but it was too late now to move.

"Hey everyone. Sorry, I'm late. There was a slight incident outside that kept me." Drew glanced at Kate as he arrived at the table. He slid in beside her.

Of course, he was joining them, Kate thought as she reached for her water glass. This day couldn't get any worse.

"What did you do to your hand, dear?" Jill asked, reaching for Kate's right hand.

"Oh, well, um…" Kate stammered. She didn't exactly want to tell her she had just been in a fight outside the restaurant. What would they think of that?

"Our Kate here just saved me from my ex-girlfriend." Drew smiled at her. He was going to enjoy watching her squirm a bit over this.

"How do you mean?" Jill had taken her napkin and dipped it in her water glass and began sponging blood off Kate's knuckles. "Were you in a fight?"

"It wasn't my fault!" Kate blurted out.

"Well, I should hope not." Jill continued dabbing her knuckles, but a smile was starting to form.

"So, who did you punch anyway?" Ken was trying to stifle a smile behind his hands. "We raised a lot of boys, Kate. We know what knuckles like that mean. Did you break their nose?"

"I think so," Kate replied in a quiet voice. "but I was just protecting myself."

"And Drew, too, from the sound of it," Peter interjected.

Ken sniggered as laughter took over. Kate's head jerked up to see everyone laughing, even Fiona. Before she could stop herself, she snorted out her own laughter.

"She just kept coming at me. I just wanted to stop her, so I popped her in the nose. It was sort of just automatic. I didn't mean to break it."

Jill looked at her son with a raised eyebrow, "Drew, maybe we need to have a conversation about the company you keep."

"No, we definitely do not need to do that, Mom. She's my ex-girlfriend for a reason. I'm pretty sure Kate has given her all the discouragement she needs to finally realize it's over."

The group quieted as the waitress approached to take their orders.

"We'd love to come by the store after lunch, Kate," Jill said as they sipped on their drinks. "I want to pick up a few small things for some of my girls for upcoming birthdays. I saw a few necklaces the other day that caught my eye. Do you mind?"

Kate looked at Fee but couldn't communicate as well as she'd like with both Jill and Ken opposite her. Fee, however, had no reservations.

She looked at Kate quickly and answered before Kate could open her mouth. "That would be fantastic!"

Chapter 28

The group moved down the sidewalk on their way to the store. Kate had been surprised when Drew had stayed. She had expected him to leave after lunch.

He had been ignoring her for a few days now. Even today, he seemed to keep his distance. He wasn't his usual joking self with her. She wasn't sure what had brought on the change in his behavior, but she was glad. At least that is what she tried to tell herself.

Even now she tossed a casual look over her shoulder, drawn to check on what he was doing. He was deeply engrossed in a conversation with his father. The two men had their heads close together and brows were furrowed. She wondered what was so important.

Drew quickly looked up and caught her eye and their gaze locked. She tore it away as she felt her stomach give a small flip. She didn't need to find herself flat on her face in front of everyone, but there had been something in that look that had taken her breath away momentarily.

"How did your store come to be, Kate," Jill asked, breaking into Kate's thoughts of Drew.

Kate began telling her about how she had come up with the idea for Seascapes when she was a teenager and worked hard towards that goal for many years. "It has always been my dream to own my own store."

"That's amazing! You overcame quite a bit to get to where you are today. The Lord has surely blessed your life."

Kate looked at her in disbelief. The Lord had blessed her life? How was that even possible given all she had gone through. Didn't a blessed life mean no hardship? She'd had her share of difficulties to overcome. She certainly would not call her life blessed. Maybe now, but not the previous years.

"If you say so." Kate stopped short of rolling her eyes, but she made it obvious she didn't share Jill's sentiments.

"Kate, you might not be able to see it right now, but the Lord has blessed your life. Just think about what could have happened to you."

Kate thought she had been doing just that. After all, she could be dead at her mother's hands. She could have died of some horrible accident or worse while her father was off on one of his binges. The attacks in the streets could have ended up with her being dragged in an alley and assaulted, ending up with more than just bruises or a cut lip.

She could have avoided all that if she had been able to stay with the Grant family. She certainly had thought of her past, repeatedly. Dwelling on the what if's had only kept her feeling miserable. Instead, she had learned to push it all to the back of her mind and just look at the here and now. It was the only way she could function.

Jill continued, "You survived what your mother did to you. Your sister wasn't as fortunate."

At Kate's startled look, Jill gently said, "Yes, we know about your sister."

Fiona broke in, "I know you've mentioned a sister, but what happened?"

Kate sighed. She was so tired of reliving the past. But Fee was her best friend. She knew she could trust her with the knowledge.

"My mother went to a locked psychiatric facility where she ended up dying from a drug overdose. She was there because she murdered my baby sister. Lori was only two when it happened. That was the reason I ended up in foster care. Well, that and the fact that my father was gone, and they couldn't find him."

Fiona gasped and covered her mouth. Kate knew Fee couldn't fathom what life had been like for Kate. She had never lived one day of neglect in her life.

Ken and Drew had caught up with the rest of the group at this point and Ken joined the conversation. "You could have gone to any other foster family in the area. Some homes weren't much better than the situations children were taken from in the first place. Instead, the Lord helped you to be placed with us."

Kate thought about this for a moment. It was true. She had begun to heal when she was with the Grants. She had even begun to thrive. That was why it had been so hard to leave and go with her father.

Jill spoke again, "I have to believe what we taught you when you were with us sustained you when you went back to your father. We know that it had to have been hard to go from a home where you were well taken care of, to one where you weren't. We prayed the skills we taught you would help you."

"They did help, and it was hard. I missed you all so much when I left. I used to try to figure out how to find you, but I didn't know how to get from Baltimore to Florida. I wasn't sure I could find you if I did."

Fee put an arm around Kate's shoulders and hugged her, offering comfort. She was still reeling a bit herself after learning about the true reason Kate had been in foster care when she was small. She couldn't understand why some parents hurt their children.

Ken spoke up, "Everything you have gone through so far has helped form you into the person you are today. From where I sit, you seem to be a well-adjusted, successful young businesswoman. Am I wrong?"

Kate tried to process the conversation. How was it possible? She was struggling to understand how all the bad things that had happened to her could have actually been good for her.

"I just don't understand," Kate finally said, voicing her thoughts. "How could all the things I went through as a child be good for me? How is that even possible?"

Maybe this had been a bad idea. She felt like she had been ambushed again but she hadn't told them no after Fiona had invited them to see the store. It felt like she was on a rollercoaster of emotions.

"Do you know what the Bible says about this, Kate? Do you remember?" Ken asked gently.

Kate just shook her head. With a shaking unsteady hand, she finally managed to pull the door open. She held it as everyone walked in.

She hoped the store would perhaps distract Ken and Jill from continuing the conversation. She wasn't sure she was up to it right now. Not after the fight she'd had with her father earlier today or the physical fight she'd found herself thrown into the middle of with that Lucy woman. How much was one person supposed to deal with anyway?

"Well, this is just lovely!" Jill exclaimed as she held up one of the newer necklaces Kate had just made a few days earlier.

Kate sighed with relief. It appeared the store had distracted everyone. She hoped it would continue as they looked around. She didn't want to have this conversation now. In truth, she never wanted to have it.

She couldn't believe a good God would have allowed her to have suffered so much at the hands of those who were supposed to protect her. How was that loving? How was that just?

Chapter 29

"Kate, do you want to talk about what happened once you were taken from us," Jill asked with concern in her voice. She had been wandering about the store looking at various things. "Sometimes voicing our hurts and hardships makes it easier to deal with them. They lose their hold on us when we can say them out loud instead of holding them in our hearts."

"I hadn't talked about those years before to anyone and yet, just in these past few weeks I started telling Fiona about some of it. I had those memories pushed as far back in my mind as they could go. But maybe you're right. I think you have a right to know."

"Let's go down to the church to talk. It will be more private." Peter made the offer quietly from off to the side where he was standing and listening.

"What if someone walks in like I like to do?" Kate didn't want to be sitting in the sanctuary sharing her past with the Grants and have other community members listening to her. What if someone like Mrs. Johnson came in? That would be awful.

"We'll use my office. The church is left unlocked during the day so people can come and go as they'd like. Some, like you Kate, come in and enjoy the windows. Some like to come and just sit in the quiet and meditate. My office is private enough that no one should bother us there."

"I'll stay here and finish up what we had been working on until Nancy comes back from her break," Fee said. "She should be here soon. Then I'll go look for sea glass or stay here and work. No worries. I've got you covered." Fiona smiled at her friend as she made the offer.

Kate walked to Fiona and, in a very uncharacteristic move, reached out to hug her friend. "Thank you," she whispered in her ear.

"For what?"

"For being such a good friend to me. I don't deserve you, Fee, but I'm so glad I have you." Giving her another squeeze, she stepped back and headed for door with the Grants.

She stopped at the entrance. Drew was still standing in the store watching them all leave. "You can

218

come if you'd like. You're a Grant, too." She surprised herself with the offer.

She saw Drew exchange a quick glance with his father and then Peter. What was that about?

"Thanks, but I think I'll head out to get some errands done. I don't want to intrude. I think you all need the time together without me there." He headed out the front door and hurried down the sidewalk.

Kate wasn't sure how she felt about Drew leaving. She didn't want to have to keep repeating her story, but she wasn't sure she wanted Drew to hear it either at the moment. She decided she couldn't deal with it right now and walked out the door with the rest of the group to go to the church.

There wasn't anything more than a few walks and cups of coffee between her and Drew currently. He had been making himself scarce the last few days anyway. She just needed to focus on what was in front of her and that was figuring out how much to share with the Grants.

What should she tell them? Should she explain how devastated she was the day she was taken away from them? Would they want to know how she had cried herself to sleep for almost an entire month after she'd left? Or how it was over a week before she would even talk to her father at all about anything? Should she share it was only about two months before he left her alone?

Her life had been full of such misery from the time she had left their house until the time she had left her father's. She thought she'd had her life under control. She thought it was all going the way it should until that necklace had shown up.

Then the package of sea glass appeared followed quickly by her father. Her quiet and peaceful life had been anything but for the last few weeks. Add to that the graffiti and the fight and she was amazed she was still functioning.

She was starting to wonder why her father had sent those things. She didn't understand why he hadn't just sold the necklace and sea glass. If he needed money, that would have been the fastest way to get some. It wouldn't have been a lot, but it would have been something.

All these thoughts swirled through Kate's mind while they walked to the church. Entering through the front, they headed down one of the side aisles to the small door Peter emerged from whenever Kate visited.

Down the hall they entered a comfortably appointed room suited for a pastor's office. She hadn't been in a lot of church offices, but in her mind it worked. The wall behind Peter's desk had a floor to ceiling bookcase crammed with books. There were even papers tucked on top of some of them. Additional piles of books were on the floor. It was obvious Peter had a love of books and a lack of shelf space for them.

A huge wooden desk dominated much of the space directly in front of the bookcase. A large leather office chair was positioned behind it. In front of the desk were two comfortable armchairs, the type one could sink gratefully into and enjoy a talk.

There was another seating area on the other side of the room. It contained a matching sofa to the chairs, which was situated in front of a bank of windows overlooking the side lawn of the church. A squat coffee table held its place in front of it.

Peter moved the chairs in front of his desk around to face the sofa. He gestured for everyone to take a seat as he asked, "Coffee?" Both of his parents simply nodded their answer.

Off to the side, Kate spied a coffee maker. It was obvious this was not the first time Peter had hosted a group of people in his office. His movements were efficient as he set about making a pot of coffee.

Soon everyone had a steaming cup of aromatic coffee in their hands. Kate knew it would soon be her turn to talk. They had all been making quiet conversation about the weather and the beach while they waited for the coffee to finish brewing. Now it was time. Her stomach was in knots and she was beginning to regret her decision to let Fiona stay behind at the store. She could have used her support.

"We know how hard it must have been for you when you were taken away from us, Kate," Ken began. "We've already told you how hard it was for us. However, we still had each other, and you were put into a situation where you didn't know anyone. You were too young to remember your father well. I'm sure the adjustment period was very hard on you."

He paused to gather his thoughts before continuing, "But I think there's something more going on. Do you want to talk to us about it? We just want to help you and we'll do all we can."

Kate knew they all deserved to know the truth of what had happened once she had left. Even though she had tried not to, she did remember how loved she had felt when she lived with them. It was the only thing that had helped her get through some of those long lonely nights.

Keeping her eyes on her hands, she began to tell her story once more. She had thought she would never tell anyone and yet in the last few weeks she'd told it at least twice. It didn't get better with the telling, but somehow became just a bit easier.

She kept her eyes down the whole time. She didn't think she could stand to see the looks of pity on their faces. She didn't pity herself. She wished she hadn't had to live the life she had, but she hadn't asked for any of it.

She had been a child and didn't have the ability to direct her own life. She had lived her life at the whim of the adults around her. Now she had control of it, and she meant to keep it. She certainly wasn't going to allow anyone, least of all her father, to change that.

By the time the coffee had grown cold, Kate was done. She hadn't taken more than a sip or two while talking. It was only now she dared to take a quick glimpse up.

Tears were running down everyone's face except her own. She was surprised to see the sorrow on not only Jill's face, but also Ken and Peter's. She knew her story could be hard to hear. It had been hard to live, but it was the past. It couldn't be changed now.

It was at this point Kate had a realization. They truly had missed her and were glad to have her back in their lives, just like they had told her. It seemed as if they really were as hurt by her return to her father as she had been.

At the time, she had thought they didn't care, but maybe they had held themselves back in order not to make it worse for her. Looking back at the situation with an adult's vision instead of a child's, she could only imagine how much worse it would have been if they had cried or fought to keep her with them. Perhaps they had fought for her like they had said.

"Kate," began Ken, stopping to clear his throat. His voice cracked with emotion. "I am so sorry, so very sorry for what you went through. I wish there was a way I could go back and change things. I wish I could have protected you like I wanted to. I thought of you as a daughter. We had the repeat assurances of the court that your father had reformed. He wouldn't give up his parental rights and they wanted to reunite you with him. They thought that was what was best for you. I'm so sorry that wasn't the case. I wish there was something else we could have done. Will you please forgive me for not protecting you?"

Chapter 30

Kate looked at Ken in disbelief. "I don't understand. Why would I need to forgive you? You didn't do anything wrong."

Kate was so confused. Why would she need to forgive the Grants? They had done everything they could for her. It certainly wasn't their fault the way her father had treated her. The only person at fault was him.

"Forgiveness is always about righting wrongs and not keeping a score card. I must believe deep down you're as angry at Jill and me as you are at your father. You might have vague memories of living with your mother, but you were so young when you came to us. You grew up in our home. You were such an outgoing and vivacious child once you became comfortable with us. You lit up our lives."

Jill nodded in agreement with what Ken was saying. She sniffed and reached for a tissue to blot her tears. "We love you so much, sweet girl."

Ken continued, "When you left, a piece of our family left, too. Our hearts were broken for years. In fact, until we heard from Peter how he had found you, our hearts never felt whole. It was almost as if we had a wound festering all this time. It was not knowing where you were or how you were doing. We finally have you back again and feel as if that missing piece is back."

Jill sobbed into her hands. She was nodding her head up and down to convey her agreement with her husband.

Kate looked at Peter. He had told her he remembered her when she first figured out who he was. His face was wet with tears as well, but he was smiling and agreeing with his parents.

Ken waited a moment as he gathered himself and wiped his face before he continued. "You were so much older when you went back to your father. Can you honestly tell me you weren't angry at us, and that you transitioned easily into life with your father? From what you have just told us, we know that isn't true."

Kate closed her eyes. No, it hadn't been easy to adjust to the life her father had for her. She had been so far out of her element there. She'd had to learn street smarts quickly to survive the city. The neighborhood would have eaten her alive, otherwise.

"Life has been so hard for you, Kate. I wish I could take all the pain you have experienced away from you. I wish…no, we both wish…no, we *all* wish you had stayed a Grant forever. I can't tell you how often, and how hard we have prayed for you."

Jill broke in, "Kate, all that Ken is saying is so true. I have prayed for you every single night you have been gone. There has always been a small piece of my heart missing. It was you. You were that piece."

Ken continued, "I see such anger inside of you, anger that wasn't there when you left all those years ago. I fear it is eating you up inside. Do you still have nightmares?"

Kate looked stunned at the question. "Yes. How did you know? I had them so bad in college the administration made me go back to counseling since I had a full scholarship. I kept waking my roommate up. They've gotten better, and I hadn't had one in months until my father came back. Now I seem to have them every single night."

With a soft smile Jill said, "You had them when you were with us, too. You were in counseling before you left, and it was working. Honey, Ken is right. We do want your forgiveness. I so wish I could do anything to take away your pain. I hate to see you struggling again."

"There is really nothing to forgive, but if it makes you all feel better, I will," Kate said, still sounding a bit confused by it all.

At this answer, both Grants looked at each other in a way only those who have been married a long time can do, but said nothing. Kate wondered what that was all about. She had forgiven them like they had asked, and she felt strangely better for having done so.

"Kate, thank you so much for opening your heart to us today," Ken said as he leaned forward and patted her knee. "I know how hard it must be to talk about your past like that. I think you should understand something though." He glanced again at his wife and son before continuing, "Forgiveness is not only something you can give all of us today, but it's also something you should think about for yourself."

At this statement, Kate looked even more confused. "Why would I need to forgive myself? I haven't done anything wrong. All of my life I was affected by choices made by other people." She was growing annoyed at this outrageous statement.

"Forgiveness isn't just something you need to extend to others, but it's sometimes something you need to give yourself as well. Sometimes we get in a self–destructive mindset. I know you say that you haven't done anything wrong, but subconsciously we can begin to believe everything that has gone wrong in our lives is directly related to our own actions."

Jill smiled and reached out to take Kate's hand. Kate allowed her to hold it briefly before pulling away. She was beginning to feel confused and angry again.

Jill took continued, "You said what happened to you was the direct result of others and you're right. As a child you had no control over what your mother did to you or to your sister. You were simply a child who thought the adults in her life were there to help her. Instead, they hurt you. All children are born believing adults are there to help them until an adult comes along to change that belief."

That's for sure, Kate thought. Until she lived with the Grants, she had no idea parents could be loving towards their children. In fact, because of how she was treated by her parents she doubted she would ever have children of her own for fear she would act the same way.

"You also had a short time in your life when you lived with us. During those years with us, we hope you learned what a healthy family looks like. We hope you learned that some adults keep their promises. We also hope you learned what it was to be safe and loved. Unfortunately, you then had more adults come along and change things for you again." Jill smiled sadly at Kate as she finished speaking.

Kate thought of her father. He had treated her in the exact opposite manner. He never kept a promise. He had never kept her safe. He certainly had never shown her she was loved.

Ken took over the conversation, "My question for you though is this, did you think it was the direct result of other adults making decisions for you or was there some small part of you that believed you were the cause?"

Kate stared at him in astonishment. Until he had voiced those thoughts, she had never been able to put it into words, but he was right. There had always been a small part of her that thought if she had been a better child, her parents would have loved her and not hurt her. If she had obeyed better, been prettier, or something. She didn't know what, but she realized she had spent years trying to figure it out.

She was angry at all the adults who had seemed to constantly change things in her life without her consent. It had started with her mother who had taken away a sister Kate only knew from stories told to her by others.

Kate had never had the chance to get to know her sister. She didn't know her likes or dislikes. She had never had a chance to fight with her over toys or share whispered conversations after the lights were out at bedtime. She realized a huge part of her missed her sister, a sister she'd never been given the opportunity to love.

She was also furious at all the people responsible for bringing her father back into her life all those years ago. In fact, just thinking about it made her begin to shake with repressed anger.

How could they have taken Kate away from the only family who had really loved her? It was so unfair how they had just stepped in and ripped her away from the Grants. She had loved them so much. They were her parents in ways her biological parents had never been.

And her father. She could not even begin to express her anger at him. It was not only for the way he had treated her when she lived there. She was also furious at how he thought he could just waltz right back into her life like nothing had ever happened.

How dare he! He had no right to be a part of her life. He had given up that right long ago. The moment he began to leave her alone with no food and no money was the moment he had ceased to be a father. No, that wasn't right. The moment he had left her to the abuse of her mother was when he had ceased to be her father.

"Kate, dear," Jill said gently as she touched her on the knee, "do you understand there is nothing you did to deserve any of what happened to you?"

"Not until you just explained it to me. I think there was always a small part of me that thought if I had been good, none of this would have happened."

Ken smiled. "Now for the hard part."

"What's harder than what I've been through?"

"Forgiving them."

Chapter 31

Drew relaxed on his couch and watched the sunset outside. His thoughts were racing as he remembered the day. First, he had the confrontation with Lucy. Then Kate had punched her.

A wide grin spread across his face at that particular memory. Kate had defended herself well against Lucy. He was pretty sure Lucy had never thrown a punch in her life, but Kate certainly had.

Most women wouldn't have punched. They would have scratched, bit, or pulled hair. Or if they had thrown a punch, they would have broken something. Kate had ended up with bruised and scratched knuckles that might be a little sore, but she hadn't broken anything. It appeared her accounts of life growing up in the rough parts of the city of Baltimore had equipped her well for self-defense.

His mind shifted from the fight to the whispered conversation he'd had with his father as they had walked to Seascapes after lunch. His dad could always pick up when someone needed to talk.

He had drifted behind the group and pulled Drew with him. "What's going on, son? What's troubling you?"

Drew shook his head even now. It was his dad's superpower. He had poured out his heart to him in those few minutes as they had walked. He had told him how he was starting to feel about Kate, but that he also felt God telling him to wait, to pull back.

"I'm having a heart and head battle, dad. My heart wants to pursue Kate, but my head is telling me to listen to God."

"That's always a difficult one isn't it? Why do you think God has those verses in the Bible? Do you remember the ones I'm thinking of?"

"Do not be bound together with unbelievers; for what partnership have righteousness and lawlessness, or what fellowship has light with darkness."

"You got it. Nice to see all those Bible drills paid off."

Drew smiled at his dad. He had hated them at the time. They had spent many Saturday evenings around the dining room table working on learning the Bible and verses.

He had been so much older when he had arrived and had known nothing about the Bible. He also hated to lose so he had spent a lot of time learning the verses and where they were in the Bible so he could win.

Once Ken had learned about Drew's spirit of competition, he had created a leaderboard for the wall. Drew had put in time whenever he could to learn the books of the Bible and memorize verses. He wanted his name on the top. The day he had finally succeeded had felt like the best victory ever. His name had stayed there until he had moved away from home.

Ken brought him back to the current topic. "Why do you think Paul reminds the Corinthians not to be yoked with an unbeliever?"

"Because he's a killjoy?" Drew laughed. "Just kidding. Probably because he knew that an unbeliever could easily turn a believer away from God instead of a believer turning them towards God."

"Exactly. So, what's your best course of action then?"

"Prayer. And lots of it. There's something special about her, isn't there?" Drew had looked up at that moment to see Kate glancing back at him. Their gazes had locked, and he hadn't been able to look away.

"I'll pray, too. It seems like you could use all the help you can get." Ken had clapped a hand on his shoulder and laughed.

Now Drew focused on that look. If his dad hadn't put a hand on his shoulder, he was sure he'd still be rooted there, just staring at Kate. He was surprised his eyebrows weren't singed from the heat in that gaze.

He had left the store to do some walking and thinking shortly after that. Even though Kate had invited him to join all of them at the church, he felt God nudging him out the door for some heart to heart conversation with the One who has the best plans for him. He had walked for over an hour, praying all the while.

He still felt something inside him urging him to continue to pray. "Okay, God. I hope you're up and listening. I need some help. Big time."

◊ ◊ ◊ ◊ ◊

Kate curled up in her favorite chair in her living room. She held a cup of tea cradled in her hands as she watched the sunset. She preferred sunsets to sunrises only because it meant she could enjoy the beauty without being up early.

She sipped her tea and thought back to the look she had shared with Drew earlier today. She was pretty sure it had stopped her heart for just a moment. Sighing, she continued to relive it for a bit longer.

She still didn't know why he had suddenly disappeared. He had been popping up everywhere around her it seemed and then he was just gone. She had been getting used to him and had started to enjoy time with him. Then, poof.

Shaking her head, she decided she was too tired to figure it out right now. Instead, she picked up the Bible Jill had given her earlier today.

Jill had saved it all these years. Somehow it hadn't been with Kate's things when she had left to go with her father. She had looked for it when she was unpacking all those years ago but hadn't been able to find it.

She had great memories of the Bible drills the family used to do on Saturday nights. She had just gotten to the point where she could stand first for a few when she found herself living her dad.

All the memories she had pushed away were coming forward. She realized it was too hard to stop them and had been trying to learn to embrace them. No matter how hard it was.

She stroked the soft leather cover of the Bible. She even lifted it to her nose and sniffed. A feeling of security washed over her. There was such safety and comfort attached to this book.

Peter had already suggested the book of John, which Kate had finished reading. Setting down her drained cup of tea, she let the Bible fall open. It landed in the book of Psalms on chapter twenty-three. She began to read the familiar words.

Memories of learning some of the verses came flooding back. She could picture the family sprawled around the living room as Ken had read to them. She could see them at the dining room table, arms overhead holding their Bibles waiting for the verses to come so they could see who would be the first to find it. She also remembered the time she had been first to stand and, in her eagerness, she had knocked her chair over backwards.

A small smile curled her lips as she continued to read. Memory after memory flooded into her mind. The smile faded as she remembered a conversation with Jill shortly before she had left their home. She had forgotten all about it until this moment.

Jill had been trying to explain what was going to happen. The pain hit Kate again as if she had just had the conversation today. It had been excruciating to leave all she could remember behind for a future with a man who called himself her father, but one she could barely remember.

Memories washed over her. It had been years since she'd allowed herself to go this far back in her past. The pain was overwhelming. It had been easier to push thoughts of the Grants to the far back of her mind, so it didn't hurt so much. Living with her father had been about survival.

She continued flipping the pages of the Bible. Maybe she could find comfort in its pages once more. Nothing else had been working. Would this?

Her eyes lit on familiar verses in John. It was the first one she had ever memorized. It was in the third chapter, verses sixteen and seventeen. She backed up to the start of the chapter and began to read slowly.

Did God love her? Was it really as easy as these verses made it seem? She thought back to when she had memorized the verses, highlighted in pink in her Bible.

Ken had the kids place their names in the verse. Kate did the same thing now as she whispered it aloud. "For God so loved the world, that He gave His only begotten Son, that if Kate believes in Him, she shall not perish, but Kate will have eternal life."

Kate closed the book and held it to her chest. Did she believe it? Did she truly believe all that Peter had been teaching her through the stories in the windows? Did she believe in a God that had always felt so far away?

A smile covered her face as she realized, she did. Peace like she had never felt before began flooding her at the realization. "Thank you, Lord. Thank you for loving me."

She continued talking to him in prayer as she drifted to sleep, with the Bible still clutched to her chest. Although, she slept in a chair, she had no nightmares that night.

Chapter 32

How do you like living here, Kate?" Jill was helping Kate put together a new display. She and Ken had joined Kate at the store this morning. Kate knew they just wanted to spend time with her, and she was finally okay with that. After her prayer last night, she was embracing having a family again. It was no longer scary. She had no more major reservations.

"It's really been a great place for me. It's calm enough in the winter and off season. It's downright chaotic in the summer. We have a lot of seasonal residents and tourists who come to Haven then."

"We loved it here," Jill responded, "when we started taking the kids. It was a long drive from Florida, but so worth it. We didn't start doing that until a year or so after you had left us though." Jill reached out a hand and touched Kate's face gently. "We missed having you with us."

Kate reached up and covered Jill's hand with her own and leaned into the touch. "Thanks. I missed you all as well. I think now that I'm seeing you again, I'm realizing just how much I did."

Kate stepped away and continued working on the display. While being touched was getting easier, she still wasn't completely comfortable with it.

"I came to the village soon after college. I knew I wanted to own my own store one day. In fact, I went to college and majored in business management. I really like the creative aspect of it, but I also enjoy supporting all the local artisans. I sell a lot of local work on consignment in my store."

"Tell me more about the jewelry you make."

"We try to use as much glass as we can find on the beaches here. We can't always keep up with the demand, especially in the summer, so we do purchase some as well. I hate doing it but it's the only way we can continue to have enough product to sell throughout the season."

"I love finding sea glass on the beach." Jill held up a necklace made of white sea glass to admire. "It can be so hard to find. I can't imagine finding enough to make the types of things you girls do." She placed the necklace back down as she spoke. "Did you find or buy this color? I've never seen it before."

"I found that one. When I buy sea glass, I try to get the more unusual colors like lavender or red."

"I didn't even know it came in other colors! I've only found white and brown and occasionally some green. I would love to see some examples. Do you have any in stock right now?"

"I do. The hardest part is finding enough of one color and in similar shapes to make matching sets. That's why we often have to buy colors. I like to put together sets. Like this."

Kate held up a set to show Jill. It was the large piece of blue sea glass she had found earlier. The glass was almost the size of her thumbnail. For the color, it was huge. She had matched it with a set of smaller pieces she'd also found and made into earrings. All of them were wrapped with thin gold wire. The wire was the smallest she used. It was one of her new favorite sets.

"Oh…. how lovely," Jill said as she held the box in her hand to look closer. "You have a wonderful skill at turning what many people overlook into something beautiful."

"I wouldn't say that. Sea glass is coveted by many the world over. Lots of other people do just what I do. It's nothing special."

Ken broke into the conversation at this point, "But it is, Kate. It really is. Not everyone can do this. Not everyone does what you do. You have a unique ability which God gave you, a special talent. You are using your abilities and talents not only to run a successful business, but you are helping others by selling their creations as well as your own. It is a true gift from God."

Kate blushed slightly. She had never looked at anything she did as a gift. It didn't feel like a gift. It was just what she did. There was truly nothing special about it. Was there?

Kate was beginning to become uncomfortable with all the praise. She wasn't used to it. She knew others liked what she offered. Some came back year after year to buy new pieces from her.

She wandered over to where Fee was working at making more jewelry leaving Jill and Ken behind to exclaim over her artistry. Just as she reached Fee, she heard a noise. It sounded like someone had come through the back door. It couldn't be Nancy. It was too early for her shift.

Fiona raised one eyebrow, "Maybe it's Drew. Go check."

Kate headed towards the storeroom. They really needed to start locking the back door. Before she could get there, however, the door that separated the spaces opened and Kate's father appeared.

She stalked towards him and quietly, but in a vicious tone of voice, whispered, "What are you doing here? Didn't I make myself clear earlier? I don't want to see you ever again. Now leave!"

"Kate, I just want to talk. I'm not leaving until you hear me out. I'm doing this twelve-step program and I need your forgiveness. I need to make this right between us. I'm clean now. I haven't gambled in over a year." The words rushed out before Kate could interrupt him again.

"I don't care! Why should I care?" Kate could hear her voice begin to rise and worked to quiet it. She didn't want the Grants to notice what was going on. It was too much to have to continue dealing with her loser of a father.

"Kate, honey, honest. I've changed. As God is my witness, I promise. I'm a different man."

"I told you not to call me honey and I don't believe you! You've said that very thing more times than I can count. Every time you would come home, I would worry if you'd had a winning streak or not. Do you know that sometimes I went days without any food because you were too busy off drinking and gambling any money you had? You didn't think about me then. Why should I care that you want to be part of my life now?" Kate said all this in a whispered shout, trying desperately to keep her voice down, but having more trouble doing so the longer her father stayed.

"Kate, is everything okay?" Ken had noticed the conversation from across the room.

"Yes," Kate bit out between her teeth. "This man was just leaving." She whirled around and started towards the front of the store. She hoped that would be enough to get her father to take the hint and leave. She knew she couldn't walk out like she wanted to, not with the Grants there thinking everything was fine.

"Kate, I'm not leaving. I'm your father. Talk to me," he called after her.

She stopped, her face growing white. She didn't even turn to look. She could tell by how quiet everything had become that everyone had heard him. There was no more hiding the fact he was here or who he was. What was she supposed to do now?

Kate heard footsteps moving across the store. She hoped it was her father heading to the door. She closed her eyes and waited to hear the door open and shut.

Instead she heard a man's voice saying, "Hello, I'm Ken Grant. It's nice to meet you."

Kate couldn't believe this. Ken was introducing himself to her father. What next?

"This is my wife, Jill. We've never met, but we were foster parents to your daughter when she was younger. We just came into town to visit our sons who live here and found Kate after not knowing where she was all these years. Isn't God amazing?"

Kate watched horrified as Ken walked closer to her father. What would her father do in the face of meeting the Grants? Would he put on his fake charm or would he turn mean? Kate wasn't sure. She might have once been able to predict his behavior, but if he had truly changed, she didn't know what he would do.

"Weren't you the ones who wanted to adopt my daughter?"

"Yes, we did. We love your daughter very much. We would have very much loved having her as our adopted daughter. Instead she was able to be reunited with you. God works His blessings in mysterious ways!" Ken answered with a joyous laugh and reached out to shake the other man's hand.

Kate watched in amazement as her father reached out a tentative hand to shake Ken's. Was her father telling the truth? Had he changed?

"I guess I owe all of you some thanks and an apology, too. I never should have taken my daughter away. She would have been better off staying with you. I see that now. I see a lot of things differently now. It's why I came back to see Kate."

Kate's mouth dropped open. She watched in disbelief as her father turned once more to her.

"I was telling the truth, Kate. I never meant to hurt you. I'm sorry. I'm so sorry for all the ways I neglected you and didn't protect you when you were growing up. I didn't know how to cope with what your mother did to Lori. It tore me up that I had no idea what she was doing to you two girls."

Kate couldn't believe this was the same father she had known. She watched as her father swallowed hard, pulling himself together so he could continue.

"I felt so responsible for little Lori's death. I wanted to make it right by trying to raise you, but I couldn't cope with the guilt and shame of the past. I started drinking again and even gambling to try to cover up the pain. But along the way, I hurt you so badly. I know

I don't deserve the right to ask, but will you forgive me?"

All eyes in the store turned to where Kate was standing in shock. Her father apologized. It even sounded sincere. Was this what it meant to follow Jesus? This felt like a miracle. Could she trust her father again?

Jill stepped up beside her and put an arm around her waist. "Would you like me to pray with you first?"

Kate looked at her. Pray. Yes, pray. That's what she needed. Her mind was whirling, and she couldn't seem to settle or even pull herself together enough to say anything. She nodded shortly.

Jill bowed her head and began. She felt Ken and Fiona closing ranks around her, close enough so they could each place a hand on her shoulders. She felt another hand reach out and tentatively place fingertips on her forearm. Kate cracked open her eyelids and saw her father standing in front of her, touching her, with his head bowed and eyes closed. She quickly closed her eyes and listened to Jill.

"Dearest Lord, we come to you today to ask for help for our dear, Kate. We know things have been hard for her, especially lately. Her life has not been easy. We ask today for you to redeem her life. Turn the bad that has happened into good as you have promised to do. Give her the strength and the courage to forgive her father. Give us the words to help lead her on that path. Lord, please give her the strength now to overcome all she has gone through. In your name we pray. Amen."

They all lifted their heads. Kate's father quickly backed up a step as he dropped his hand away. He looked at Kate, searching her face for any hope that she might forgive him.

Kate breathed deeply. She had thought another panic attack would have hit by now. Instead, she felt peaceful. She felt a love for her father she had never felt before either.

Opening her mouth, she said, "I forgive you." Then felt calmness sweep over her as smiles spread across all the faces in the room.

Chapter 33

Drew whistled as he walked to the church. Today was going to be a good day, he thought to himself. The sun was shining. The birds were singing. Okay, now he was just getting corny. He chuckled as he continued, heading to meet his parents and Peter at the church.

He had thought his prayers would help ease the thoughts of Kate, that he wouldn't be dwelling on her so much. Instead, the opposite was true. He was thinking about her more than ever.

He stopped whistling and began praying quietly out loud. "Okay, God. We've been having conversation after conversation. So, what's going on? I like her a lot. Like, a lot. You know this. We've talked about it."

Thoughts of her eyes and hair and… He broke off the train of thought and kept walking and talking. "What gives? Lord, if you want me to move past this relationship, then you've got to help me out here and get her out of my head. If you want more to happen, then you need to let me know. And soon. I'm not sure I can continue this way, God."

As he approached the church, he glanced off to the side where there was a small park. He and Peter had worked to clean out all the debris under the large pine tree growing there.

They had raked all the old needles and pinecones and put in a crushed shell walking path along with a few benches. They had even created a few small flower beds for some color. No one had really been using it though.

There was someone sitting on one of the benches today. As he got closer, he realized it was Kate. He stopped and whispered under his breath, "Is this my sign, Lord?"

He changed course and walked towards where Kate was sitting. She hadn't spotted him yet. Her head was bent as she sat and read a book. She was biting her bottom lip, which he found utterly adorable.

He stepped onto the path and the noise of his feet crunching the shells brought her head up to see him approaching. A smile crossed her lips but faded quickly.

"Hey," he said.

"Hey, yourself," she replied and waited.

He couldn't seem to do anything but stand and look at her, drinking in the sight of her. He had missed their walks on the beach and their coffee dates.

"Did you need something?" She closed the book and laid it beside her on the bench. "I think your parents and Peter are inside if you're looking for them."

Drew glanced down at the cover of the book and felt his stomach flip. It was a Bible. Could God really be answering his prayers? It might not mean anything, but it did mean she was searching. Maybe.

"What are you reading?" He picked the Bible up, holding it in his hands as he sat beside her.

"Your mom gave that to me a few days ago. She said it was mine when I lived with them."

He rubbed a hand over the cover. It looked similar to the one he had. "Do you mind?" He held it up, asking for permission to open it.

"Go ahead," she nodded.

Sure enough, there was a similar inscription inside the front cover as there was in his own. "To Katie, may these words never return void. Read them and allow them to seep into your spirit and lead you every day of your life. Love Mama and Papa."

"So, are they?" He looked at Kate as he waited impatiently for her answer.

"Are they what? What are you talking about?"

"Are the words leading you?"

"Yes, yes they are. Finally."

A grin spread across Drew's face. "How about a walk on the beach?"

Kate looked at Drew. He had ignored her for days but now he wanted to start taking walks with her again. She wasn't sure she wanted to play this type of game. She wasn't even sure she wanted to get to know him better. Did she?

She decided to be direct for a change, "Why have you been ignoring me?"

Drew was slightly startled at the question, but she deserved to know why. He hadn't kept his interest in her a secret.

"How much have you read so far?" He asked as he handed the Bible back to her.

"Some. I've finished the book of John. What does that have to do with it?

"So, you haven't read anything that Paul has written? Nothing in first or second Corinthians or Ephesians or anything there?"

"No, should I?"

254

"No. Well, yes, eventually. But you don't have to read it all in one sitting," he answered with a grin. "I only ask because it may help to make sense of why I pulled back."

Drew had never been this forward with a woman in his life. He felt continued nudging from the Holy Spirit, so he dove in.

"I like you, Kate. A lot. I want to get to know you better, but I'm not the type of guy who dates to date. I'm looking for a commitment. A forever commitment."

Kate felt a blush begin to build. Maybe she shouldn't have asked him in the first place. Was he going to tell her she wasn't good enough for him? That they couldn't date because he was a Grant? She wasn't sure and she didn't have a lot of experience. She'd never had a long-term boyfriend and had only gone out for a few casual dates over the years. Dating had never been a high priority for her.

"You need to know that Paul talks about our situation in second Corinthians. He talks about how a believer shouldn't be bound or committed to an unbeliever. Kate," he reached out and held her hand in his, "I pulled back because I was starting to fall really hard for you. And until I knew for sure you were a believer, I had to wait. God was calling me to wait and to pray. And that is what I did."

Kate looked at their entwined fingers. It felt nice. She felt a wave of warmth flood her at their grip. She looked up into his eyes.

"How about that walk then?" Kate asked as she rose and tugged on their clasped hands.

Drew's familiar grin was back. He winked and said, "I thought you'd never ask."

Chapter 34

Kate was trying to stay focused on Jill and Ken. They had joined her this afternoon on the beach to look for sea glass. She knew it was just their way of spending time with her, but she was okay with that. Fiona had practically shoved her out of the door before lunch to go with them when they arrived.

They were walking along Kate's favorite stretch of beach with their heads down, looking for a sparkle of sea glass. There were multiple tide pools and sometimes Kate would come here just to look through them. Finding sea glass was just a bonus.

Today she was having even more fun since both Grants were having a great time on the search and discovery. They were almost like little kids discovering new things.

Jill was the next to shout. "Ohhhh…look at this! It's a sea star! Is it okay to pick it up do you think?"

Kate laughed, she had been doing a lot more of that lately as well, "It's fine, but just don't keep it out of the water long. I'm surprised you know the correct name for them."

Jill reached down and gently lifted it out of the water. "I love learning about God's creation. It's so fascinating! For instance, did you know that if one of these creatures loses an arm, they can regrow a new one?"

"I did." Kate continued scanning the ground nearby looking for good pieces of glass.

"Did you also know that if part of their central body, this part right in the middle, were to be detached from the regular body, just part of it, it could regrow a completely new sea star? Isn't that amazing?" Jill was so delighted in each of the creatures she had been finding and had been spouting facts like this to Kate the entire time. Kate was having fun though. This was one of the most enjoyable days she'd had in quite some time.

The now frequent walks on the beach with Drew were becoming a favorite part of each day. He had started bumping into her again on purpose to invite her for walks.

"Check out this one," Ken held out his palm with a large, frosted white piece of glass sitting in the middle of it.

"How beautiful!" Jill had taken the piece from Ken's hand and was admiring it while holding it up to the light.

"I can show you how to make it into a necklace later if you'd like," Kate offered. She was enjoying getting to know Ken and Jill better over the last few days.

"I'd love that! What was it that drew you to sea glass?" Jill pocketed the piece of glass and started walking slowly again beside Kate, searching for more.

"It was actually my biological mother." Kate was finding it easier and easier to discuss her past. She finally felt like she was healing.

She went on to share the story of the heart shaped necklace with Jill and Ken. She even mentioned how it had turned up at her store. "My father must have left it when he came into town. He was the only person who could have had it," Kate finished.

"I would love to see it," Jill said. "I've never seen red sea glass before."

"I'm not sure I still have it. I told Fee to throw it away. I didn't want to see it again. We can head there now and see if she listened to me or not."

Kate realized the red sea glass necklace no longer had a hold on her. She was wanted and loved. Her past didn't have to continue to dictate her worth.

Kate caught Jill and Ken exchanging a look she couldn't interpret. Did they know something about the necklace and sea glass collection showing up? She shook her head slightly. That was ridiculous. How could they?

Fiona greeted them as they arrived back at the store. "So, find anything good on the beach today?" she asked.

"Ken found this great piece of white glass. Kate offered to show me how to make it into a necklace," Jill grinned.

Fiona glanced at Kate and saw the slow smile filling her face. She realized Kate had never truly seemed happy in all the time they had known each other. Content perhaps, but not happy, not like this. Now Kate seemed to almost be glowing with joy. She smiled more readily and seemed to enjoy spending time with people.

Of course, Fiona had also seen the way she looked at Drew. More importantly, she saw the way he looked at her. There were sparks flying there and she couldn't be happier for her friend.

"Hey, Fee, did you toss out that red heart necklace like I asked you to?"

Fiona was startled. After the necklace had appeared Kate had told her throw it away. Fiona hadn't been able to. She had stashed it in an out of the way place hoping Kate would want to see it again someday.

"Um, yeah, I couldn't throw it away. I hid it in the back. Did you want it?"

"Yes, do you mind getting it? I want to show Ken and Jill."

Fiona quickly disappeared into the back room. She wanted to get it before Kate changed her mind.

Kate heard the front door and turned with a smile. She knew it would be Drew. He had been stopping by the store every day. Since she hadn't seen him yet today, she thought he would be by soon.

"Hey there," he said as he walked towards her.

"Hey yourself." A large grin covered her face.

Drew stopped when he heard a throat being loudly cleared. He looked up to see his parents looking at him. "Oh, hi! I didn't see you two there."

Jill looked between Drew and Kate and said, "Obviously not. Anything you want to tell us?"

"Not a thing."

At this moment Fiona returned with the necklace, "Here it is! Did I interrupt something?"

"Nope. What do you have there, Fee?" Drew headed towards her hoping to fend off any curious inquiries from his parents. He would tell them things were developing between Kate and himself when the time was right. The time was not right while they were all standing in the middle of her store.

Fiona set the box on the counter and everyone crowded around to see the necklace. She pulled the top of the box off slowly while glancing at Kate. If she had to dive for a bag to help her friend breathe, she wanted to be ready.

"Oh my, that is simply gorgeous!" Jill reached out a single finger and touched the pendant.

"Is this one of your new creations, Kate?" Drew was curious about the unusual necklace.

"No, it was my mother's. She used to wear it every day. I have vague memories of playing with it when she held me." Kate reached out and picked it up.

"I do have something else to show you," Fiona said. "Do you remember the box of sea glass that came after the necklace?" Fiona looked uncomfortable in asking. She was afraid of upsetting her friend.

"I remember," Kate replied. She wasn't reacting at all like she had when the items had first appeared. She knew it was because she now felt loved and wanted, not just by the Grants either. She shot a glance at Drew and smiled.

"Well, I've been working on some pieces this week while you have been out of the store. Do you want to see them?"

"Absolutely. I'd love to." Kate smiled at her friend as Fiona hurried back to the storeroom.

She came back with several necklaces draped over her wrists and one fist clenched closed, obviously holding some smaller pieces. She grabbed a piece of black velvet and began laying everything out.

It was obvious she had been busy. She had made at least a dozen necklaces and a few even included matching earrings. The pairings were also set apart due to the rareness of the color of the glass used in each setting. In fact, Kate knew some people would ask if they had made the glass themselves in order to get the colors they used.

Fiona had also added silver and gold beads to many of the pieces. It was obvious she had been working hard on each one. She had an eye for detail and each one showed her creativity. Some were made with gold wire and others with silver. However, she had made quite a few with copper wire as well. It was not a type of wire they used often, but it set off some of the colors nicely.

"I wanted to make some of these signature pieces and create something beautiful. I had some gold-filled wire on hand to try. It is a bit more expensive than some of our regular wire, but I thought they would sell well this summer when the tourists are here. I also used a lot of the tarnish resistant sterling silver. I love how these came out. What do you think, Kate?"

Kate walked closer to the counter and picked up each piece to examine. She didn't say anything as she held each one up and turned it this way and that, looking at each one from every angle. Finally, she set down the last one and turned to Fiona.

"Fee, you did an amazing job! I love them all! I think we should do more with the gold-filled wire. I love how it makes the colors pop. The copper is also so pretty. That's becoming a popular look right now. Excellent work!"

Fiona sighed with relief and smiled at Kate. "You had me worried there for a minute! I thought for sure you were going to tell me to take them all apart, scrape the wire, and start over!" She laughed. "I'm so glad you like them."

"You do really great work, Fiona," Jill said. "How long does it take you to make each one?"

"Well, it depends on the shape of the glass and the wire I'm using. Generally speaking, each piece probably takes about thirty minutes. If it's very delicate work, it may take a bit longer to finish."

"I have never seen colors of sea glass like this before," Ken said. "Did you find them on the beach we were just walking on?"

"No, these were from the package of sea glass Kate's father left a few days after the necklace." Fiona reached out to adjust a few of the chains.

"Are you sure it was your father who left the packages?" Ken asked with a look of concern.

"Who else could it be," Kate said. "I have no other siblings. My mother is dead. I don't know where all these things went after my mother died. I do know she used to wear that necklace all the time. I think she had the glass, too. I assume my father had both. It wouldn't make sense for anyone else to have it."

Ken and Jill exchanged another significant look. Kate caught it and this time didn't let it pass. "What? What aren't you telling me?"

Chapter 35

It's probably nothing, but Kate, you did have another relative," Ken said hesitantly. "Your mother's mother was alive when you came to live with us. She was extremely unhappy about you being placed in our home. In fact, she petitioned the court for guardianship. When she was denied, she promised to never be a part of your life."

Kate broke in, "I thought she was dead. My father told me I had no grandparents or other relatives."

Ken continued, "I don't know if she's still alive or not, but she was when you were young. She was angry about not getting custody. Apparently, there were some questions as to whether she could care for you properly. There had been allegations against her in the past for harming children. Nothing had ever been proven, but since your mother had just been institutionalized for harming you and, of course, what she had done to your sister, the authorities didn't want to take any chances."

Kate was stunned. She had always believed the only living relative she had was her father. Whenever she had asked him about grandparents, he had told her they were all dead. He had lied to her. Again.

Jill picked up where Ken had left off. "We also learned she used to visit your mother every week when she was in the state hospital. Your mother's behavior always escalated afterwards. After her death, there was some suspicion it was your grandmother who slipped your mother the pills she ended up overdosing on."

Kate was having a hard time taking in what Jill and Ken were telling her. Her grandmother helped her mother kill herself? What was so wrong with her family they treated each other this way?

"Since no one knew where your father was located, the chances are good the necklace and sea glass collection actually had gone to your grandmother, not your father." Jill reached out and patted Kate's hand. "Are you okay, sweetie? We know this is a lot to take in on top of everything else that has happened."

Kate could feel her knees begin to shake. She made her way to a stool and collapsed on to it. She had a grandmother. Aren't grandmothers supposed to be kind, white-haired, little old ladies who baked cookies for their grandchildren and spoiled them? Obviously, her grandmother didn't fit that stereotype any more than her mother had fit into any type of maternal mold.

"Why was I never told any of this before?" Kate asked in a shaking voice.

Jill reached out to stroke Kate's hair. "When you were staying with us, the caseworker refused to tell you and made us promise not to say anything until you were older. We had been discussing telling you for quite some time and then your mother died. At that point we began to work on finalizing your adoption and just figured we would tell you once everything was final and you were safely with us with no chance of anyone taking you away."

Kate put her head down on the counter and breathed. How could a good God allow so much to happen to her? Where was the justice in any of this? Why would an innocent child have to endure so much? Questions continued to swirl as she worked to stave off the rising panic attack.

She felt another hand on her back. She glanced up to see that Drew was standing beside her. He was rubbing small circles of comfort. "You okay?"

"I don't know. I just don't know right now."

"Then your father came back, and things became hectic," Ken picked up the story. "We didn't realize until just now that you didn't know. We just assumed your father would have told you."

Kate let out a harsh laugh. "My father told me all my grandparents were dead."

Jill continued to stroke Kate's hair as she picked up the story. "Maybe they are at this point. Maybe he didn't lie. We just know what we were told all those years ago. Something could very well have changed since then."

Kate sucked in a deep shuddering breath. Jill was right. Maybe her father hadn't lied. Maybe her grandparents were dead, all of them, like he had told her. If so, it would be one of the only truthful things her father had ever told her.

Kate raised her head, "It's okay. I never knew I had a grandmother. It doesn't matter anymore. I'm fine," Kate said again. She realized she really was okay. The panic had begun to recede.

The initial shock of finding out she had a grandmother who had potentially been just as abusive as her mother was wearing off. She was an adult now and there was nothing this person could do to harm her. She was not a helpless child anymore. She could stand up for herself and not allow anyone else to have sway over her life.

The bell tinkled as Nancy opened the front door and walked inside. She stopped at the sight of all the people standing there. She looked at the Grants and a change came over her. "You!" she hissed. "What are you doing here?"

Fiona spoke up quickly, "Nancy! What is wrong with you? These are friends of Kate's who are here visiting."

"I know who they are," she continued in a hate filled voice. "They're the ones who kidnapped my granddaughter from me. They're the ones who stole my blood, my own flesh and blood, from me!"

Chapter 36

I don't understand," Kate said. "*You're* my grandmother? Why didn't you ever say anything?"

Nancy turned towards Kate, "When that weak daughter of mine couldn't control herself and killed Lori, I wanted to take you into my home. I would have raised you to be stronger than she had been, but the police and the caseworkers didn't see it that way. They stole you from me. They had no right! You're my flesh and blood and no one else's!"

Unseen, Fiona slipped out past Nancy who was too focused on Kate to notice. Kate saw her go and hoped she was going for help. Even with Jill, Ken, and Drew here, she didn't feel entirely safe. It was obvious Nancy was having some type of mental break. How else could you explain all she had done?

"You sent me my mother's necklace, didn't you?" Kate was surprised to find her voice holding firm. There was no panic. There was just a feeling of strength and she knew it was because of those who were there with her. Ken, Jill, and Drew had closed ranks around Kate. Knowing they were there helped give her courage to continue to confront her grandmother.

"Of course, it was," Nancy spat viciously. "If your father had ever gotten his grimy hands on it, he would have sold it long ago."

"And the box of sea glass?"

"Yes! That is *my* collection. I know how rare some of those colors are. It gave me a bit of pleasure to know you have your love of sea glass from me. Your mom only wore the necklace because I made her. So weak. She always did what I told her to." Nancy continued as if she was almost talking to herself.

Fiona quietly returned with one of the beat cops who patrolled the Main Street of the village. A slight shake of Ken's head stayed them from speaking. Nancy was so caught up in her speech she hadn't heard or seen them return.

Nancy was almost unrecognizable as she continued to spew hate at everyone. "I convinced my daughter the only decent thing she could do was kill herself and rid this world of her weakness. It was so easy to slip those pills past the guards. Stupid people only look for what they think is there. It was easy to hide them in my locket."

Kate wanted answers. She knew this might be her only chance. She needed to keep Nancy talking. "How did you find me?"

"It was hard after my good for nothing son–in-law ran off with you. Did you know he wasn't just trying to keep you from these people?" She flicked a derisive hand at Ken and Jill. "He was also trying to keep you from me. He didn't want me to have anything to do with you."

Kate was beginning to realize maybe her father had been trying to protect her at some point. He might not have done a good job at it, but it seems he had tried to some extent.

Nancy continued to rant at Kate, "Just when I figured out where he had taken you, you were off to college. At that point I knew I couldn't do much and I just waited. I'm good at waiting. One day the time would be right."

Kate didn't know what she meant. Right for what? She never thought she'd be thankful for not knowing her relatives, but right now she was grateful she had never known this woman when she was a child.

Nancy continued to tell her story. "I had to work hard to find you after college. I didn't expect you to move out of the Baltimore area. Once I found you again, I applied for the job, and that was when I knew for sure you had no clue who I was. You didn't even blink at my name. I found that to be pathetic. No one had ever bothered to tell you about your grandmother!"

"Why did you come here?" Kate questioned again. "I don't understand why you decided to hide who you were? What was your purpose after all of these years?"

"I had no purpose other than to be near you for now. You were my granddaughter. I could see you were weak though, just like my daughter. I was waiting until I could show you how strong you could be.

"Did you spray the graffiti on the store? Was that you?"

Nancy ignored the question and continued with her ranting. "That was until *those* people came here." She pointed at the Grants with a sneer on her face. "I knew they were going to take you away again. I was working on a plan to stop them. Then that pathetic excuse for a son–in–law showed up. I knew I would have to wait again. There was no way I was going to let him back into your life either. I would kill you first!"

At this point, the officer made his presence known. "Ma'am, I need you to come with me. It sounds like we may have a few issues to clear up, including the threat you just made to this woman."

Nancy, upon hearing his voice, whirled around and screamed. She bolted for the back of the store. She moved like a much younger woman. The officer raced after her while the rest of the people in the store looked on with mouths opened.

"This has to be the craziest day I've ever had," Fiona said with a shaking voice. "*That* was your grandmother?"

"Apparently so, but I guess we'll have to wait and see what the police say." Kate suddenly burst out laughing. All the Grants and Fiona began talking at once.

"Kate! Are you okay?"

"What is so funny?"

"What is wrong, honey? Are you alright?"

"Kate? Kate! Stop it!" Fiona's voice broke out above the rest and Kate tried to pull herself together.

Still chuckling she tried to explain what she thought was so hilarious. "It is just that...well...I have no other relatives. My mother was mentally unstable and tried to kill me. My father was a drunk and a gambler who neglected me throughout the time I lived with him. And now my grandmother. Ha! Definitely not the…" she began to chuckle again, "cookie baking variety, is she?" Once more she broke out into howls of laughter.

Slow grins started to spread across everyone's face. They began to laugh along with Kate. Fiona was relieved her friend seemed to be handling the situation well. Normally something like this would send her into a panic attack. The opposite seemed to be happening instead.

Laughter rang out throughout the store as Kate made her own observation. She may not have chosen to be born into the family she had, but she was certainly glad for those she had picked to be her family, the people in the room with her right now, laughing with her.

All heads turned as the bell over the door chimed and Mrs. Johnson entered. "What is going on? I have never seen such unprofessional manners in my life. Young lady, this is not how one runs a store."

Chapter 37

Sunday morning dawned bright and early as Kate made her way to Peter's church. She was looking forward to the sermon this morning. She smiled to herself as her thoughts turned towards Drew. He was doing worship again this morning and he had hinted at a surprise for her this week.

Her smile grew wider as she remembered last night. Peter had come over to Kate's apartment to visit. Kate knew he was really there to check on her after everything that had happened with Nancy. A small chuckle escaped as she recalled how nervous he had been when he brought up the fact that his parents would be hearing him preach.

"I haven't been this nervous since I preached my very first sermon." Peter was pacing back and forth in Kate's small living room while he talked. "This is ridiculous! I have even preached this sermon before. It was years ago, but it seemed like a good time to share it again. I just don't understand why I'm so nervous! I always seem to get nervous whenever they hear me preach." He had flopped back on to the couch opposite of where Kate was ensconced in her favorite armchair.

Kate had laughed at him. He had given her a wry smile in return. "I think it's hilarious. I've never seen you act like this."

"Well, welcome to the real me. I am human after all!"

"You've always come across as so confident whenever you've shared your Bible stories with me. I'm not sure how I feel about human Peter versus Pastor Peter."

"First, you're stuck with human Peter from now on." Giving her a smile, Peter leaned forward suddenly sounding more serious than ever and continued. "And second, these are not just *my* Bible stories. They are stories for everyone. The Bible shares with us God's words. Everything in the Bible is inspired by God. In fact, the book of first Timothy tells us that all scripture is 'God breathed.' Do you know what that means?"

Kate shook her head as Peter continued. "It means that while God Himself did not physically write each word, He inspired each writer. The Bible in and of itself would just be words without that. Every word in the Bible was given to the writer by God. We are to use it for teaching, learning, and even rebuking or discipline. To believe one word of the Bible is true is to believe it is *all* true. There may be different authors attributed to each book of the Bible, but the overall author is God Himself."

"I've never heard that before. How is that possible? Didn't Moses and Paul live at different times, even centuries apart? How did God inspire the authors?"

"Well, in biblical times, the Lord spoke to people through dreams and visions. It's recorded in the Bible several times. He also came and spoke directly to a few, such as Moses in the burning bush. Do you remember that story?"

"I think so. Moses was supposed to go save the Israelites from the Egyptians and God came to him in a burning bush to give him his orders. Right?"

"Essentially, yes, although you are missing a few key principles. Keep reading that Bible. God still speaks to people today, but just not usually in fiery shrubbery. While he could certainly do that since nothing is impossible for God, he typically uses other means and methods."

"You said if you believe one word of the Bible is true, you have to believe it's all true. Why is that? I've heard people talking before about the Bible and they seemed to pick and choose which parts worked best for them." Kate had been enjoying her time with her Bible. She had even skipped ahead to the books Drew had mentioned the other day.

"Unfortunately, that can happen. God lays out His plan for how we are to live our lives clearly in the Bible. He tells us what a sin is and how to avoid it. Needless to say, it gets pretty uncomfortable if someone like God is telling you *not* to do something and yet you continue to do it. It can be easier to say it might work for other people, but not for yourself."

Kate nodded her head. She could understand that. No one liked being told they were wrong. She was beginning to understand more about why Drew had pulled away from her. She smiled as she thought of all their walks together lately. She was enjoying getting to know him better. She listened as Peter continued.

"That is why I said if you believe one part of the Bible, for instance, that Jesus came to earth as an infant, lived and died, and yet rose to life again on the third day in order to pay the penalty for your sin, than the rest of the Bible needs to be true as well. Otherwise Jesus came for no reason at all. All the Bible must be true to give any credence to why God sent his Son here to earth.

"Kate, what do you believe? Do you believe God's word is true?"

"I do. Did you know your mom had my old Bible after all these years? I've been reading it every day. I like it better than the Bible app I was using after you told me to start reading the book of John."

"I didn't know that. What do you think?"

"I think I've been missing more than just having you all in my life. I've missed having God there, too."

Peter grinned. "Fair warning, I'm coming in for a hug. You'd better be prepared!"

Kate laughed as she stood to greet him in the middle of the room. She was getting used to all the hugging the Grants did.

Peter pulled back and looked at Kate. "I'm so glad we found you. You're our little lost lamb."

Chapter 38

Kate arrived at Peter's church earlier than normal. She smiled thinking how happy she was to be able to walk there on autopilot. She'd been spending enough time there that she no longer needed to concentrate on her destination once her mind knew where she was going.

Looking up, she glanced off to the left. Standing at the corner of the building was none other than her father. She wasn't sure why he was there but started walking towards him to invite him to come to the service with her. She supposed she needed to start somewhere in trying to repair their broken relationship.

Suddenly, she glanced to the right. Standing on *that* side of the church was her grandmother! She stopped dead in the middle of the sidewalk.

Her grandmother was so busy glaring at Kate's father, she didn't realize she had been noticed by others. Two police officers were coming up behind her. Kate just watched to see what would happen.

"Do you think she'll stop long enough to notice what's going on?" A voice spoke in Kate's ear causing her to jump and whirl around.

Fiona was behind her chuckling. "Sorry! Wow, you should have seen your face!"

The officers had almost reached their intended target at this point. She watched as her grandmother spotted the officers just before they reached her. She screeched and raced off. It was obvious the police didn't want to tackle an aging woman, but when it became apparent she was going to outrun them again if they didn't do something quickly, one tackled her to the ground.

The panting officers soon had her handcuffed and hauled upright. They each grabbed an elbow and marched her towards their vehicle. Amazingly enough, Kate realized she felt pity for her grandmother.

Fiona put a hand on her shoulder. "You okay?"

"You know what, I really am. Let's go get my dad and find a seat."

Kate recognized she hadn't fared better than her father in some regards. While she didn't have any obvious addictions, she'd lived a life full of pain and anger. Kate considered how the hurt in her father's past had driven him to addiction and wondered what had happened in her grandmother's past to make her who she was today.

Kate suddenly realized how grateful she was. She could have easily turned out like her mother or even her father. She had been abused and neglected but hadn't done either of those things to others.

Instead she'd lived her life the best way she knew how and determined from this day forward, her past would no longer control the person she was. She was going to live a happy life, one without fear!

Fiona reached over and threaded her arm through Kate's. "Your grandmother must run marathons or something. I've never seen a sixty-something year-old woman move that fast before!"

Kate joined her in laughter as they headed toward her father. The smile stayed on her face as she approached him, "Do you want to join us?"

A slow smile spread across his face, "I'd love to."

The three climbed the stairs together. Kate was looking forward to hearing Peter preach. If she could catch his eye, she hoped to make a face or two at him as well, just to see if he were as nervous as he had seemed the night before. After all, what were sisters for?

Chapter 39

Fiona and Kate, with her father in tow, quickly found the Grants seated near the front on the left side of the church. Kate liked this side of the church the best. It was where she'd sat the first day she had come here so upset about the necklace. Now, all these weeks later, she still found herself coming to the church for solace and comfort.

As she slid into the pew beside Jill, she reached over for a hug. This was becoming second nature as well. Kate had never been an overly physical person, but now she found she didn't mind it quite as much as she'd once thought.

"How are you today, sweetie?" Jill smiled as she sat back.

Kate relayed to her all that had transpired outside. Chuckling, she shared how her grandmother had yet again tried to run off.

Ken reached across to shake Kate's father's hand, "Nice to see you here, Bill."

"Thanks, it's nice to be in church."

Kate realized that her father had changed, just as she had, through God's amazing grace.

Drew stepped to the microphone in front of him, caught Kate's eye and sent her a wink. "Let's all stand and sing together." He strummed a few notes on his guitar and the congregation broke out into song.

Amazing Grace, how sweet the sound
That saved a wretch like me
I once was lost, but now am found
Was blind, but now I see

Kate realized in that moment she had been like the wretch the song talked about. She had been lost and had needed God in a way she had never thought about before. She knew in that moment she had been a sinner who needed to be saved by God's grace.

T'was grace that taught my heart to fear
And Grace, my fears relieved
How precious did that Grace appear
The hour I first believed

Kate realized her fears were gone. It's was the first time she could remember not having some fear hanging over her head. The peace it gave her was something she'd never felt before in her life.

Through many dangers, toils and snares

I have already come

T'was Grace that brought me safe thus far

And Grace will lead us home

Kate knew that if ever a song was written for her life, it was this one. She had lived through all types of dangers and only through God's grace had she survived.

At this point, Kate realized she was crying. Tears were streaming down her face. She was shocked. She hadn't cried in years. She had learned to stuff her emotions in order to protect herself.

She stopped trying to sing and just listened to the lyrics. God *had* been good to her, so very good. He saved her from death as a child and from neglect when she was older. She had restored her to the Grants, and she was again part of a family that loved her. She couldn't believe how fortunate she truly was.

Glancing over, Fiona saw Kate's distress. She quickly put an arm around her and whispered in her ear, "Are you okay? Are you upset about your grandmother earlier?" Her whispering caused Jill to glance over.

Jill instantly became concerned as well and leaned in. She whispered a similar question, "Are you okay, sweetie?"

"I am. I'm just realizing how truly blessed I am."

Everyone laughed softly as the hymn singing was ending. They knew they would need to wait until after the sermon to celebrate.

Kate sat down as Peter stepped up to the pulpit. She smiled widely at him to encourage him. Maybe she'd forget about giving him a hard time after all.

Chapter 40

How about a walk?" Drew had approached Kate at the store the next day.

"I thought you'd never ask." Kate laughed as she called out to Fiona. "Are you good?"

"Yes, yes, yes. Get out of here you two. The new girl starts this afternoon. I can handle it. See you later!"

Kate threaded an arm through Drew's, and they headed out the door. He had started showing up every day around lunch and they would go for a walk. She would have to give Fiona a bonus for all the extra time she was putting in right now.

"Three Cat okay with you?" Drew looked down and thought about how lucky he was to have found her.

"Absolutely. I love Three Cat."

"Is that all you love?" Drew stopped on the sidewalk and turned to her. "Do you love anything else?"

"Drew Grant. What are you doing?"

"Just having a conversation. Why?"

She shoved him gently as she laughed. "It sounds like more than just a conversation."

"Well, since you asked," Drew pulled her close. "There has been something I've been meaning to tell you."

"Well, I never!"

The couple broke apart to see Agnes Johnson standing in the middle of the sidewalk glaring at them.

"What type of behavior is this? And in broad daylight in the middle of the day. You should both be ashamed of yourselves. Why, in my day…"

Drew cut her off, "In your day, Mrs. Johnson you would have been cuddling with your husband if you had the chance, too. I heard he was one handsome fella."

Kate stared at the sidewalk. Not because she was embarrassed, but because she was trying desperately to hide her grin. Drew was charming Mrs. Johnson and she found it hilarious.

"Well, yes, yes, he was, but still."

"I promise we won't do anything you wouldn't have done, Mrs. Johnson." Drew winked at the woman and saw a slight blush stain her cheeks.

"I suppose that will be fine. Now, about the music at church…"

"Mrs. Johnson, I would love to have that conversation with you at some point, but Kate and I are late for an appointment. Can we do this later?"

"Of course, I'll make an appointment with your brother and you can join us. Have a nice day."

"How did you do that?" Kate was duly impressed.

"Do what?"

"Get Mrs. Johnson to back down like that? She usually comes into my store and steamrolls me."

"It's all about the charm. Now, I think we were talking about the things we love."

"Hey, Drew!"

He groaned as he lowered his forehead to Kate's. "I lost that thought."

Kate laughed lightly as they pulled apart again to see who had called out this time.

Peter was jogging toward them down the sidewalk. "Did I interrupt something?" He raised an eyebrow at Drew.

"Nope. What do you want, Peter?" Drew shot his brother a look that clearly stated that whatever this interruption was, it had better be good.

"I wanted to let Kate know that I ran into Jordan Smith this morning while I was walking to church."

"What does the chief of police have to do with this, Peter?" Drew was starting to glare at his brother.

Peter shot a glance back. "Well," he drawled out the word since it seemed Drew was in a hurry for him to leave, "he wanted to pass on a message to Kate and asked me to give it to her. They found the person who vandalized your store."

"Really?" Kate was surprised. "I thought my grandmother had done it. If it wasn't her, who did it?"

"Lucy Reynolds."

"What?" Drew was shocked. His ex-girlfriend had done all the damage to Kate's store? She was crazier than he had thought.

"Who's Lucy Reynolds?" Kate didn't know the name. She had no idea who this person was, and why she felt the need to deface her store and break her window.

"It's Drew's ex-girlfriend. The girl you punched outside the Three Cat Café. That is Lucy Reynolds."

"But she damaged my store before I punched her. Right? Why would she do that?"

Drew sighed, "I'm pretty sure it's because she thought we were dating."

"We are dating. Aren't we?" Kate's eyes had a sparkle of mischief in them. "Or are you just leading me on Drew Grant?"

"We're dating. Absolutely. But we weren't then. She just thought we were."

"Well, no harm done now. Everything is fixed and we are now apparently dating. Will she have any charges against her?" Kate wasn't sure how it all worked.

"That's what Jordan wanted to know. He asked me to have you swing by the police station and either press formal charges or drop them. Do you know what you'll do?"

"Not really. Any advice for me, Pastor Peter?"

"You can certainly extend forgiveness. I think she's pretty embarrassed to have been arrested and booked. It will show up in the paper."

"Forgiveness. I think I like that idea best. We'll head there now and do that. Thanks, Peter."

"Do you guys want to come over for dinner? It's mom and dad's last night. They've been here long enough and need to head out to the next visit before someone thinks they're playing favorites."

None of the Grant kids ever felt like their parents played favorites. Ken and Jill loved all their kids equally, no matter how they were added to the family.

"We'll be there. Now scram. We were in the middle of something." Drew smiled as he shoved his brother away.

"I thought you said I wasn't interrupting anything. Well, I can certainly tell when I'm not wanted. I'll see you guys tonight." He turned and headed back to the church.

Drew pulled Kate close again. "Now, where were we?"

"You were telling me about all the things you love, I think."

"Oh right. I love the Three Cat Café. And I love pistachio ice cream."

Kate pulled a face. "Blech! Pistachio ice cream? Really?"

"No, but there is something else I love. You."

Kate's eyes locked with his as his face lowered. "Are you okay with that, little lamb?"

"Absolutely," she breathed as their lips met.

To the Reader

Thank you for picking up my book and taking the time to read the words I wrote. I appreciate that. I hope you enjoyed the story. I hope it challenged you and inspired you. It certainly did me while I was writing it.

I wanted to share with you the Bible references for the stained-glass windows. I encourage you to go read them for yourself.

The story of Christ's birth can be found in Matthew chapters one to two. More widely known is Luke chapter two. Both give different perspectives of the same event. Don't let the familiarity of the story stop you from seeing the miracle it contains.

God sent His only Son to earth to save you. He would have done this for just one person, but He did it for everyone, including you, dear reader.

The story of the lost sheep can be found in Luke chapter fifteen in the first seven verses. I have always loved this story. It's important to note that it's not about Jesus coming to find me, a person who has already chosen to follow Him. It's a story about Jesus rejoicing over someone who has turned away from going their own way and going towards Jesus. That always brings great rejoicing!

You can read the parable about the wise and foolish builders, otherwise called "the two foundations," in Matthew 7:24-27. The words of Jesus are as profound today as they were when He spoke them centuries ago. Make sure you are one who has "ears to hear."

Our last window story may be one of the most important ones. It is also found in Matthew chapter seven. You can read it at the beginning of the chapter in verses seven and eight. You can also read it in Luke 11:9-10.

As Peter tells Kate in the story, Jesus wants to be a part of your life. He wants to come in and live life with you. He is knocking. Do you hear Him? Will you answer the door? Don't make a snap decision.

Jesus will be a part of your life once you ask Him to do so. That doesn't mean your life will be easy, but it does mean you'll never be alone again. Eternal life is yours for the taking. Reach out and take His hand.

Acknowledgements

I can do all things through Him who strengthens me.
~Philippians 4:13

This book has been more years in the making than I care to admit. It started as part of National Novel Writing Month in 2013. So, I begin there by thanking the great folks at NaNoWriMo for encouraging people to just get the words down on the page.

Thank you to those who encouraged me on this journey to finish well or just finish already! It was harder than it looked. Thank you especially to Robin Merrill, writer extraordinaire. I cherish our friendship. Your kind words and encouragement were invaluable.

To my wonderful friends, near and far, who were so excited and kept pushing me to get the job done. I want to especially thank Molly Sparling and Nicki LeBlanc for reading and critiquing and helping to find those pesky comma and word usage errors I made. If you find any in this story, they are all mine.

Thank you to my wonderful, loving husband, Bob. He beat me to publishing, which served to push me harder to finish. Not that we're competitive at all, right babe? The fact that he read this story not once, but twice, when it was far from his type of genre says loads about how much this man loves me. The feeling is mutual. Thank you for all the insight you gave me on the book, honey. It made it a better story.

Lastly, I thank God. He has blessed me with a life I never thought possible.

What's Next?

There are four more windows in Peter's church whose stories need to be told. Stay tuned for book two in the Forgiveness of the Heart series, *Haven*.

Follow me on Facebook:

https://www.facebook.com/evelyngracebooks

Check out my website for more information:

https://www.evelyngracebooks.com/

Made in the USA
Las Vegas, NV
26 August 2021

28887800R00174